Dear Reader,

This inspiring first novel, winner of the RWA Golden Heart Award*, is based on the life of a real horse.

As an experienced jockey, author Chris Platt has known her share of horses. She received her first gallop license at the age of sixteen in Salem, Oregon, and several years later received her jockey license, earning her a proud place among the first female jockeys to break into the business!

Chris jockeyed at the Salem and Portland race courses, and she also worked as a groom and trainer's assistant. Of all the horses she's known, none touched her more than the one she writes about in this book.

"The *real* Willow King's name was King Hark," Chris told me, "and he was born with legs that were so crooked the owner wanted him put down." Chris vividly recalls the day the trainer bravely told the owner, "'That colt will be just fine. You've been telling me all along that I could have any colt I wanted—I'll take *that* one!'"

What King lacked in physical advantage, he compensated for with hard work and determination. His legs eventually straightened, and he went on to win the Portland Meadows Mile and some big-stakes races, proving that the trainer's belief in him had been well founded. King Hark was all heart—and so is this award-winning story based on his experiences. It is my hope that you'll enjoy this poignant first novel as much as I have.

Alice Alfonsi
Senior Editor

*The Golden Heart is awarded annually by the RWA (Romance Writers of America), a national organization of 8,000 writers, primarily women.

Willow King

Willow King

Chris Platt

Random House Riders

Random House New York

AUG 1998

Jacket art by Joanie Schwarz
Jacket design by Georgia Morrissey
Interior design by Gretchen Schuler

Copyright © 1998 by Chris Platt
Cover art copyright © 1998 by Joanie Schwarz
All rights reserved under International and Pan-American Copyright
Conventions. Published in the United States by Random House, Inc., New York,
and simultaneously in Canada by Random House of Canada Limited, Toronto.

http://www.randomhouse.com/

Library of Congress Cataloging-in-Publication Data
Platt, Chris. Willow king / by Chris Platt.
p. cm. – (Random House riders)
SUMMARY: Thirteen-year-old Katie, who is herself physically challenged,
saves a crippled foal from euthanasia and nurses him back to health and
eventual championships.
ISBN 0-679-88655-9 (trade) – ISBN 0-679-98655-3 (lib. bdg.)
ISBN 0-679-88656-7 (pbk.)
[1. Horses–Fiction. 2. Horse racing–Fiction.
3. Physically handicapped–Fiction.] I. Title.
PZ7.P7123115Wi 1998
[Fic]–dc21 97-27846

Printed in the United States of America 10 9 8 7 6 5 4 3 2 1

Dedicated to
Buck Buchanan and King Hark,
two true champions

Author's Note

———— ❧ ————

My special thanks to my critique partners,
Tess Farraday, Millie Holland, Wanda Prukop,
and Laurie Hendricks;
my husband, Brad, for being so supportive;
and my editor, Alice Alfonsi, for having faith in this book
and getting it to the starting gate!

Willow King

⇥ *Chapter One* ⇤

"Destroy him? What do you mean 'destroy him'? He was just born!" Katie stared at the bay colt that lay nestled in the thick bed of straw. Grey Dancer, his dam, nuzzled his still-wet coat and nickered softly to him, encouraging him to stand and nurse.

Katie leaned her forehead against the cold wood of the stall door and listened to the drumming of the Oregon rain on the barn roof. The gloom of the day settled over her like a wet blanket.

Old John, the trainer for Willow Run Thoroughbred Farm, placed a comforting hand on her shoulder. "I tried, missy, but it's the boss's orders, and what he says goes. There's nothing either of us can do about it. This is a farm for racing stock. With legs like that, this colt will be lucky to stand and nurse, let alone race someday."

Katie looked down at her own legs. Where would she be if her parents had felt the same way about her at her birth? With one leg almost an inch shorter than the other, it wasn't a great handicap–but it was enough to set her apart.

1

She wiped the back of her hand across her eyes, fighting the burn of tears. She was thirteen now, too old to break down and cry like a baby. But she felt so helpless. She had no claim to the farm. She didn't live here. She was just the neighbor girl who had bugged Mr. Ellis until he had finally given up and let her help with the horses.

She pushed her long brown curls back over her shoulders and turned pleading blue eyes on the old trainer. "But it's not right, John. Look at how big he is. He's the best-looking colt foaled this season. So what if his legs are crooked? The rest of him is perfect."

"You're right about that, Katie girl."

Together they watched the colt struggle to rise. A gentle nudge from his dam sent him scurrying to stand. Legs tangled and buckled, but eventually he got to his feet, teetering as he stretched his neck to suckle.

She wished Jason Roberts could be here to share this, but he didn't even know she existed.

"Attaboy, Willow King." Katie spoke words of encouragement to the new foal. His ears flickered at the sound of the human voice and he turned his head to stare in her direction, milk dripping from the curly whiskers under his chin. But the effort was too much for him, and his legs collapsed under him like a folding chair snapping shut.

"See? He knows his name already," Katie said as she knelt quietly beside the mare and foal, intent on helping him to stand and nurse again. Fortunately, Grey Dancer was a kind mare. She wouldn't turn on Katie for entering the stall when there was a new foal inside. Many mares would.

"Don't you be namin' that colt now, Katie," John said testily. "No need for you to go getting attached to him when Mr. Ellis has ordered him put down."

Katie stood and brushed the straw from her jeans, then limped to the edge of the stall. She had forgotten to wear her orthopedic shoe this morning. Her back would pain her later, but it would be worth it. She wouldn't have missed this birth for anything.

But now it might turn into a funeral. "I'm not going to let him do it," she told John determinedly. "So what if his legs are too crooked to race? He could be a trail horse or a carriage horse, couldn't he?"

John tilted his head and settled his felt hat more firmly into place. "Now, missy, this colt's got some of the finest racing blood this farm has to offer. You think he'll ever be content to be an ordinary cart horse?"

Katie thought of her dream of becoming a ballerina. That dream had vanished when she hadn't outgrown the clumsiness of her disability. She could handle the fact that she would never be a dancer, but how would she feel if someone wanted her *dead?*

"Being a carriage horse is better than being put to sleep!" Katie exploded. She turned her back on John and helped the foal to stand. He wobbled and bobbled but soon found the food supply again and resumed sucking greedily.

"That's it, King, drink all you can," Katie urged. "It'll help you to grow up big and healthy." She knew how important it was for the foal to get that first milk from his mother. It contained all the antibodies he would need to survive and grow strong.

Katie surveyed the colt's crooked limbs. "What about leg casts, John?"

Old John took off his hat and scratched his head. "I've seen it done," he admitted. "But it's hard on the little ones. They can't run and play like the other foals when they have those heavy casts on. And the things have to be taken off every couple of weeks and tightened for them to work. Sometimes those casts do more damage than good."

Katie sighed and went back to the foal. King stopped nursing and turned his big brown eyes toward her, seeming to size her up, determining if she might be a worthy playmate once he learned how to work his legs properly. He made a faint attempt at a nicker and took a step toward her, but his legs tangled and he fell in a heap at his dam's feet.

Katie laughed at the surprised look in his inquisitive brown eyes. King floundered for a moment in the bedding, then lay back in the deep straw and closed his eyes. Only the rhythmic chomping of Grey Dancer at her hay and the chickens scratching at the dirt on the barn's floor disturbed the quiet.

"Look at him," Katie said. "He's so trusting, he doesn't even know that death is near. Isn't there anything that can help him?"

"Well," old John began as he forked some hay into the stall. "I tried to tell the boss, but he didn't want to listen. I've seen a few colts born with crooked legs. Of course, none of them were as bad as this little colt's. The best remedy I've seen is good food, plenty of sunshine, and lots of pasture to run in."

"That's it?" Katie's eyes widened in surprise. "No medicines or bandages?" That seemed far too simple to work. She wished the problem with her own legs could be fixed that easily.

"That's it," John repeated. "It's best to let Mother Nature take her course. Those legs will straighten of their own accord. Most of those colts went on to win races."

Hope fluttered in Katie's heart. "But if that's all it takes, then why won't Mr. Ellis give it a try?"

"The final decision rests with the boss, and he thinks the colt's legs are too crooked for it to work."

The sound of tires grinding on the gravel driveway announced the arrival of the veterinarian. Katie's heart sank again and her stomach felt as if a large, cold stone lay inside it.

Dr. Marvin, the stable's vet for as long as Katie could remember, ambled up the shed row, shaking the rain from his hat and coat. "Morning, John, Katie." He tipped his head in their direction. "So where is the little fella?"

Katie stepped aside, and the vet entered the stall, shrugging off his raincoat and throwing it over the door. "Not a very good day to be born," he noted as he dried his hands before picking up his instruments and beginning his examination of the colt. "But it's also not a very good day to die."

Katie heard the sympathy in Dr. Marvin's voice and

pounced on it. "Oh, Doc, you can't put him down. He could be a champion someday!"

The vet paused and turned to Katie. "I wouldn't get my hopes up that high," he cautioned. "He's got some of the worst legs I've seen on a colt.

"But," he added, "I think they might straighten enough for him to be of use somewhere."

"See!" Katie beamed, turning to John. "Now all we've got to do is make Mr. Ellis understand."

"I've already tried that, Katie," Dr. Marvin said. "It's breeding season, and having a bad-legged colt out of your prize stallion's first crop doesn't go over well with buyers or breeders. Mr. Ellis has high hopes for Beau Jest's offspring, and he doesn't want anyone to know this colt of his exists."

Katie shook her head, tossing her brown curls over her shoulder impatiently. "I didn't know he could be so heartless."

"He's really not being that cruel," Dr. Marvin said, pulling a stethoscope from his bag. "He doesn't expect this colt to be able to stand and nurse. A quick death is preferable to slow starvation."

"But he's already stood and nursed." A note of hope crept back into Katie's voice.

"He has?" Dr. Marvin's brows rose to a point in the middle of his forehead, giving him the appearance of a wise old owl.

"Yes, he nursed for about a minute."

"That's a good sign." The vet put the stethoscope to the colt's chest and listened. King shifted in the straw, and Dr. Marvin put a steadying hand on his side. "He's got a strong heartbeat, and his lungs are clear. If he could get enough milk into him to gain some strength, he would make it."

"Do you really think so?" Katie was getting more excited by the minute.

"Too bad his legs are so crooked. This is one of the best-looking colts I've seen come off this farm."

"We've got to convince Mr. Ellis that Willow King is worth saving!" Katie slammed her fist into the palm of her hand. So what if the colt had a handicap? He could overcome it.

"Here he comes now," John warned. "If you've got a plan, it's now or never, my girl."

Katie jogged awkwardly down the barn's shed row to greet the owner. Tom Ellis sloshed into the barn through the mud, his wide-brimmed hat set against the rain. Behind him a splash of yellow daintily picked its way between the puddles, a large umbrella turning back the onslaught of rain.

Only Cindy Ellis would wear her best school dress to the barn, Katie thought sourly. She and Cindy had been neighbors for the past eight years, but they could hardly be called friends. They tolerated each other, and that was about it. What was she doing here? Cindy only came to the barn when her horse was bridled, saddled, and ready to ride. Today was definitely not a day for a gallop over the fields.

"Hello, Katie. What brings you out on such a miserable morning?" Mr. Ellis's voice always sounded so businesslike.

Cindy closed her umbrella and daintily brushed at

the water spots that speckled her dress. "Yes, Katie, what *are* you doing here?"

Ignoring Cindy's curious gaze, Katie managed to get a few words past the lump in her throat. "It's Grey Dancer's foal, sir..."

"Ah, yes. She's always been your favorite of all my horses, hasn't she? It's too bad about the foal. I had great hopes pinned on that colt."

"He could still be a winner, Mr. Ellis." Suddenly, Katie lost all control of her tongue. "He stood and nursed. Dr. Marvin says he will live if he just gets some milk down him. Old John says he just needs lots of sunshine." The words tumbled out of her mouth like water over a fall.

"Hold on there, Katie. What are you getting at?"

"Please don't put Willow King down," she pleaded, looking to Cindy for help. The two of them didn't see eye to eye on too many things, but surely Cindy wasn't so horrible that she'd want to see the colt die.

"Willow King?" Tom Ellis stared at Katie. "That's a powerful name, but I'm afraid he won't be able to use it. There's no hope for that colt, Katie."

"Nothing is ever hopeless," Katie said.

Cindy stepped forward and tossed her mane of straight blond hair over her shoulders. "Are you sure, Daddy? Maybe he'll outgrow it?"

Katie managed a weak smile for Cindy. She was grateful for the help.

"No, girls. There's no sense getting your hopes up. The colt's too deformed to make it on his own. He'd take a lot of extra work, and even if he did make it, he'd still be worthless. No legs, no racehorse. You two run on up to the house now. I promise you, the colt won't feel any pain." He shooed them toward the barn door.

"Wait!" Katie yelled. She had to make them see that the colt didn't have to be perfect to be of use. "You can't do this! If it's too much work for you, I'll do it. Just let him live. Please!"

Mr. Ellis sighed and put his hand on her shoulder. "Katie, you just don't understand. No matter how much work you put into this colt, he'll never amount to anything."

But she did understand. She saw the same sentiment in her classmates' faces when it came time to choose teams in gym class. Nobody wanted to pick ol' limp-along Katie—she couldn't run as fast as the others or move as easily. She understood all right.

Mr. Ellis continued. "We could save him, but the only thing he would be good for is standing in the pasture. At best, you might be able to do some light riding on him when he's older. But this is a racing farm, not a convalescent home for hopeless horses."

Katie could tell he was at the end of his patience. If she didn't convince him now, King would be gone forever. The rain outside turned to hail and began to beat down furiously on the roof. It echoed the turmoil she felt in her heart. The colt *was* worth saving. The tears that had threatened earlier now slipped down her cheeks. Cindy was looking at her with sympathy in her eyes. Maybe she wasn't so bad after all.

Mr. Ellis turned to walk away, but Katie reached out for the sleeve of his coat, stopping him in his tracks.

"What if I buy him from you?" It was a desperate attempt, but it was her last hope.

Cindy stepped forward, the look of pity gone from her eyes. Curiosity had taken its place. "Katie Durham, how do you think you can afford to buy one of our race-horses when your mother can't even afford to pay the taxes on your farm? What will you do with a horse if you lose your land?"

Cindy's father gave her a sharp look and the girl retreated behind him, her bright yellow dress disappearing behind his gray overcoat like the sun slipping into a storm cloud.

Lose the farm? Katie wondered what Cindy was talking about. Her mother had never mentioned that they were in financial trouble. Things had been rough since her father died, but Katie hadn't known they were that bad. If that was true, then they needed King worse than ever. If he was raised right, he could become a valuable champion, like his father, Beau Jest.

Katie watched as Mr. Ellis scratched his chin and studied her. She saw his gaze drift to her leg and comprehension dawn in his eyes. He now realized why this colt was so important to her.

"Katie," Mr. Ellis began in a fatherly tone, "you don't have any money to purchase a colt. You already have one horse, and I doubt your mother would let you have another. I could give you the colt, but it's still going to cost for his vet bill."

"I want to pay for the colt. I can work it off. You know I'm a good groom." Katie jammed her hands into her pockets and kicked at the dirt on the ground, willing the tears in her eyes to stop falling.

Cindy stepped out from behind her father. Katie didn't like the look in her eye. When Cindy Ellis wore that sugary-sweet smile on her face, it spelled trouble for somebody.

"I know a way Katie can pay for the colt," she spoke in a cotton-candy voice. "You can trade your show horse, Jester, for him."

Katie sucked in her breath. She felt as if somebody had just punched her in the stomach. Not Jester! Her father had given her Jester for her tenth birthday. Cindy knew how much that horse meant to her. And to think she had been having nice thoughts about the girl!

"That's an idea." Mr. Ellis scratched the stubble on his chin. "Cindy has been bugging me to buy her a new show horse. She always complains about you beating her in the ring. Maybe she would have a chance at some ribbons if she had Jester. I'm sure your mother wouldn't want to part with such a valuable animal, but maybe you'd be willing to lease him to us for a few years? It would certainly make it easier on you and your mother if you only had one mouth to feed. Of course, this whole deal hinges on her approval."

Katie swallowed the lump in her throat. Thoughts of Cindy riding her beloved horse turned her stomach. The girl didn't have a very good seat, and she continually sawed at her horse's mouth. But Mr. Ellis had a point. If her mom was having trouble with the farm, it would be easier to care for only one horse, and once King grew strong enough to run in races, he would eventually pay his way and theirs too.

Father and daughter stood waiting for her answer—Mr. Ellis with a friendly, helping smile and Cindy with a greedy smirk. She had been trying for years to beat Jester in the show ring. Now it looked as though she would be winning all the blue ribbons on him.

Never in Katie's life had she had to make such a difficult decision. She opened her mouth and forced the words out before she could change her mind. "Okay, Mr. Ellis, you've got yourself a deal." She saw the admiration in his eyes when he reached out to shake her trembling hand. Cindy looked like the cat that ate the canary.

"You've made a good decision," Cindy bubbled as she looped her arm through Katie's and pulled her down the shed row. "I'll let you come visit Jester anytime you want."

Katie's legs felt numb. Had she made a mistake? She thought again of the little bay colt and her own mother's plight with their farm. Her instincts told her she had made the right choice, but her stomach felt as if it had dropped down to her feet.

As long as Cindy didn't ride Jester too much, he would have a good home, and Katie could visit him whenever she wanted. Certainly, by the time King was old enough to race, Jester would be back in her barn.

They reached the door, and Cindy turned and gave her a big hug. "I think this could be the beginning of a great friendship," she said.

Wreathed in smiles, with her dress billowing in the

wind, Cindy looked like a gigantic sunflower. She wanted to be friends, but all Katie wanted to do was push her into the nearest mud puddle.

Backing away, Katie turned and ran out into the cool rain. The water poured from the sky, cooling her troubled thoughts. With each step she took, the name *Willow King* rang in her ears. By the time she reached her house, she knew she had made the right decision. Now all she had to do was convince her mother.

⊱ *Chapter Two* ⊰

Katie burst into the kitchen, startling her mother, who stood at the stove preparing breakfast. The house was warm and smelled of baked bread and hot cocoa. "Mom, we've got to talk."

Peg Durham's eyebrows rose at the serious note in her daughter's voice. "Have a seat at the table, dear." She set a steaming mug of cocoa in front of Katie and sat across from her. "What's so important that you're out in the rain this early in the morning? Is it Grey Dancer? Did she have her foal?"

Katie took a sip from the mug, rolling it between her hands to warm her chilled fingers. "Are we going to lose the farm?" So much for subtleties, she thought as she watched her mother sit back in her chair.

"Who did you hear that from?" Mrs. Durham frowned, then rose, spooned oatmeal into a bowl, and stirred in a liberal dose of brown sugar. She set it in front of Katie.

"Cindy Ellis told me." Katie lifted her eyes to meet her mother's and peered into an older reflection of herself. There was no doubt they were mother and daughter. They both shared the same brown hair and blue eyes, with just a sprinkling of freckles across the nose.

"Cindy Ellis? I don't know how Cindy came by this information. It isn't her place to know about such things, let alone talk about them."

Katie watched her mother fidget with her coffee cup, swirling the spoon around and around. "But is it true, Mom?"

"Well, it's not quite that bad, but things could be better. I'm a little behind on the taxes, but with the extra work I've taken on, I might be able to get caught up in a year or two."

Katie sat forward in her chair. "Mom, I think I might have the answer to our problems." At the smile on her mother's face, she continued. "Grey Dancer had her foal this morning, and he's beautiful. I think he'll be a champion someday."

"But what does that have to do with us, dear?"

Now came the hard part. Katie took a deep breath and began. "The colt was born with crooked legs, and Mr. Ellis wanted to have him put down. Old John says that all he needs is a little sunshine and plenty of room to run, and his legs will straighten."

Her mother looked at her expectantly. "I still don't see what that has to do with us, honey."

"Mom, I want to trade Jester for that colt." There, it was out. She held her breath, praying her mother would agree. She had done all she could to arrange the deal; she couldn't bear to lose King when she was this close. The stillness of the room was interrupted only by the dripping of the water faucet.

Mrs. Durham looked into her daughter's desperate, pleading eyes. "Are you sure, Katie? Your father gave you that horse."

"It won't be permanent. Mr. Ellis wants to lease him for three years in exchange for the colt. I know he's going to be a champion, Mom. When he wins some races, we can pay off the taxes." Her hands fumbled with the napkin, twisting and crumpling it as she waited for her mother's answer.

Peg Durham took a sip of her coffee. A slight smile tugged at the corners of her mouth. "Well, I guess a little guy won't eat as much as Jester does. At least not for a year or two."

Katie flew out of her chair and threw her arms around her mother, hugging her with all her might. "You're the best, Mom. You won't regret this."

Mrs. Durham patted her arm and smiled. "I'd better not, or you'll be grounded for the rest of your life."

Katie climbed down from the school bus and went into the house to change her clothes. Earlier, she had called the Ellis farm to confirm their agreement and work out the minor details. Mr. Ellis didn't want King anywhere on the property. He was afraid that potential breeders wouldn't bring their mares if they saw the crooked-legged colt his prize stallion had sired.

Grey Dancer and her foal would stay in Jester's old stall and paddock until it was weaning time. Then the mare would return to the Ellis farm, and King would have to learn to depend on Katie. All that was left to do now was exchange the horses.

Katie took Jester's bridle off its hook and entered his stall. The horse nickered a greeting, and tears sprang to her eyes. She felt like a traitor. Jester was her first horse. He had been patient and trustworthy during her first years of learning, never balking or running off when she gave a wrong cue or pulled too hard on the bit. As she became more proficient at riding, his spirit and capabilities rose with her newfound talent. She might be awkward on the ground, but on Jester's back she could soar like an eagle. Together they had been a dynamic team.

Katie threw her arms around Jester and buried her face in his mane. She breathed in his warm scent and choked on her tears. "I'm sorry, old boy, but there was no other way." She lifted her hand and stroked the small white star on his forehead. "It will only be for a few years, then you'll be returned to me." Jester nudged her pocket. She pulled out a carrot and broke it in quarters, feeding them to him one at a time. "I'll come visit you every day. I've agreed to clean stalls and do some grooming at the farm to pay off King's vet bills and make some extra money for feed. So I'll see you almost as often as I do now. The only difference will be that Cindy will be your owner for a while."

At that thought, Katie buried her face in Jester's neck again and cried in earnest. Her heart felt too heavy to carry in her chest. Jester stood quietly, seeming to understand her need for the emotional release. When she had dried her tears, Katie pulled the bridle over his head and swung up onto his back. They trotted down the road to Willow Run Farm.

When they arrived, the farm was a beehive of activity. Mares and foals were being turned out to run in the fields, yearlings were being handled and gentled by their grooms, and the two-year-olds were being broke to the saddle in preparation for their first races in early summer.

Old John didn't believe in running two-year-olds. He said they were still growing and the cartilage in their knees wasn't closed. He blamed the breakdown and destruction of many good horses on the early races.

Mr. Ellis was just the opposite. He liked running his colts early so he could determine their potential. He wanted all his foals to be born in the first few months of the year. It gave them an advantage over the later colts when it came to racing, because they were usually bigger and stronger. At two years old, a couple of months' growth could make all the difference between a winner and a loser. And since Mr. Ellis owned the farm, he always got what he wanted.

Katie pulled Jester to a halt and patted him on the neck. "In a few more years, Willow King will be running his first race, and you and I will be leading him in the post parade," she promised. Cindy wouldn't refuse her that, she was sure.

"Katie!" Cindy picked her way through the barnyard, waving and smiling as she approached. Her long blond hair was pulled back into a French braid, and she looked older and more sophisticated than her thirteen years. She wore a pair of designer riding jeans—the kind Katie's mom could never afford—and a mint green blouse that set off the color of her eyes.

Katie felt a twinge of jealousy. Cindy had it all: she

was popular in school, she had a loving mother and father, a great place to live, and all the horses she could ever want. And now, she had Jester, too. Katie felt the burn of tears pricking her eyes again.

"I've been watching for you." Cindy reached out to stroke Jester's soft muzzle. "Oh, Katie, I'm so glad you decided to trade Jester. You know I couldn't do anything with that beast of mine. Jester is such a gentleman. I know we'll win lots of ribbons together."

Katie forced a brave face and took a deep breath, concentrating on the fresh smell of Oregon pine. She had cried enough tears. It was time to let go, though she could hear the splintering of her heart as it cracked in two.

"I'm sorry," Cindy went on. "Here I am prattling on about my good fortune, and you're losing your best buddy. What an idiot I am." Cindy smiled. "But you're getting two friends in return—me and Willow King."

Katie brightened a little at the mention of the colt. She started to dismount, but stopped as a minor commotion sounded behind her. She turned to see Jason Roberts coming across the barnyard, his long-legged stride carrying him past the squawking chickens and unmanageable colts. At first she couldn't believe her eyes, but no one else had that same shade of strawberry-blond hair and that winning smile.

"Yoo-hoo, over here!" Cindy waved frantically in his direction.

"You mean you *know* him?" Katie's heart hammered in her chest. There wasn't a girl in her school who didn't dream of Jason Roberts. He was president of the ninth-grade class, captain of the basketball team, a hunk to die for—and he was actually nice. She had admired him for many years but never had the nerve to say more than "hello" or "excuse me" when she passed him in the hall.

She was glad she had put the lift in her shoe this morning. The last thing she wanted was to have that awkward limp around Jason.

Katie wished she could just stay on Jester's back. She was as graceful as anyone up there. At least she hadn't worn her special shoe this morning. It was more obvious than the lift. The lift just slipped inside her ordinary shoe, but her special footgear had a built-up sole.

Normally, a person used either a lift or an orthopedic shoe, but her leg fell on the borderline of being too short for the lift to work well. So she also had the shoe—which she really hated. She wondered if Jason had ever heard any of the kids at school tease her.

Jason's family owned a large spread, part of which bordered the back of the Durhams' property. Occasionally, she would see him riding in the fields, but she always turned and went the other way, afraid that he might think her stupid if she tried to speak and became tongue-tied.

Besides, he was a year older than she, and ninth-graders never paid much attention to kids in the lower classes. Next year, he would be in high school, and she would still be stuck in junior high. It was a hopeless fantasy. Cindy's voice brought her back from her dream-world.

"Of course I know him. He's my boyfriend. Come on, I'll introduce you."

Katie's mouth dropped open, but she quickly snapped it shut when Jason stopped beside them, smiling up at her as he patted Jester's neck.

"Hello, Katie."

"So you two do know each other?" Cindy looked inquiringly at Jason.

Katie was shocked that Jason knew her by name. She couldn't seem to find her voice, so she just sat on her horse and tried for a nice smile, hoping that she didn't look like the Cheshire cat.

"Sure, I know Katie," Jason said. "Our properties border each other, and I see her riding through the fields every now and then." He turned his gaze back to Katie. "I've waved to you a couple of times, but I guess you never see me."

Katie opened her mouth to speak, praying that her voice wouldn't come out as a little squeak. "I'm sorry. I guess I didn't notice. I'll pay more attention next time." She hoped God wouldn't punish her for that little white lie. Of course she had seen him. She had just assumed that he'd been swatting mosquitoes. She couldn't believe that he had been waving at her.

"I told Jason about our little secret. I'm sure my father wouldn't mind. Jason is sworn to secrecy."

"On my honor." He crossed his heart and raised his right hand. "So what are you going to do now that you don't have a horse to ride?" He grabbed Jester's bit and waited for her to dismount. "It'll be another couple of years before that colt will be old enough to break–that is, if his legs straighten enough for him to be ridable."

Katie slid her hand over Jester's neck and patted him

lovingly. "Oh, his legs will be straight enough. You'll see him win the Futurity race at Portland Downs. And even if they don't straighten, bad legs won't make him useless." She punctuated her point by making a graceful dismount.

Jason looked at her and smiled. "You're right about that."

Katie had the feeling that he was talking about her as well as the horse. Her heart brightened, and she liked him all the more for it. Funny, but she wasn't so nervous talking horses to him. "In the meantime, I guess I'll just have to get used to not having Jester around."

Cindy pouted prettily, trying to draw the attention back to herself.

"Katie Durham, don't you go trying to make me feel guilty about this. We traded fair and square. Besides, I'm sure my dad will let you ride the old Appaloosa pony horse."

"And if you get tired of riding that old rocking horse, I'll let you ride one of my Paints," Jason offered.

Cindy put her hands on her hips and squared her shoulders. "You won't even let *me* ride one of your precious Paints—how come you'll let Katie?"

Jason reached out and tweaked Cindy's braid. "These are cutting horses, girl. They can jump out from under you quicker than greased lightning."

"I can ride as well as Katie can." Cindy crossed her arms and frowned.

"I know you can." He winked at Katie, flashing her a crooked grin. "It's just that I didn't figure you would want to be riding another horse for a while now that you've got a new one."

That brought the smile back to Cindy's face. "You're right. Who needs one of your ol' Paints when I've got the horse that's going to win at all the local shows. With the way this horse moves, no one can touch us in the English Pleasure classes."

Cindy didn't notice the stricken look on Katie's face, but she saw the frown that Jason gave her and laughed at him, thinking he was upset because she had insulted his horses. "Don't be an old stick-in-the-mud. Call one of the grooms and tell him I want my saddle and bridle. I'm going to ride this horse now."

Katie stood back and watched as the tack was placed on Jester. He had never carried another person's saddle before, and the bit Cindy used was much harsher than the ring snaffle bit he was used to. Cindy stepped up to the horse and pulled the girth as tight as it would go with one savage yank. Jester swished his tail and rolled his eyes, but like a gentleman, he accepted the unwarranted roughness with patience.

Despite all of her years in the saddle, Cindy had never acquired the graceful balance and good horsemanship that came with years of practice. Instead of a quick, agile mount, she put all her weight in the stirrup and pulled downward on the saddle as she attempted to climb on top of the horse. Jester shifted nervously as the saddle pinched his skin.

"Hold still." Cindy jerked on the bit and the horse's head popped up at the unaccustomed pressure on his soft mouth. "What's wrong with this horse? I've never seen him act this way before."

Jason stepped forward and pulled an extra four inches of rein out of Cindy's fingers. "You've got to give this horse a little more rein. He's not used to a heavy hand."

Katie smiled her thanks at him and advised Cindy, "Jester is a push-button horse. He will respond to the slightest pressure of your hands or legs. If you pull too tight, he'll toss his head."

Cindy looked condescendingly down at them. She had a proud way about her that sometimes made Katie feel about six inches tall. From that high perch atop Jester's back, it was even more intimidating.

"Are you guys trying to tell me I don't know how to control a horse?" She pulled on the bit and spun Jester around to face the arena. "Watch this."

Katie wanted to close her eyes as Cindy cantered into the riding ring and put Jester through his paces. She jerked on his mouth and used leg pressure that was strong enough to cue an elephant. The horse moved around the arena, throwing his head up and running zigzag patterns, trying to do as his rider asked. Finally, Cindy trotted him back to where they stood.

"See, I can ride this beauty. We've just got to get a little more used to each other."

Jason stepped up and took the reins from Cindy. "That's enough for today." He looked over at Katie and gave her a reassuring smile. "I think the two of you should go riding together a few times so Katie can give you some pointers on how Jester likes things done."

Cindy puckered up her face and started to protest,

but Jason stopped her. "Don't be stubborn, Cin. All horses are different. You want to win some ribbons, don't you? You've got to learn this horse's temperament and how to handle him if you want to do that."

"I guess you're right. This is going to be my best year in the show ring. I know Jester can carry me to high-point champion. I was just a little upset because I thought you were telling me I didn't know how to ride."

Katie finally found her tongue and stepped forward to speak. "I'd be glad to give you a few lessons."

Cindy gave her that look again, and Katie knew she'd said the wrong thing.

"N-not that you need lessons," she stuttered, trying to recover from her blunder. "You ride perfectly fine." She hoped God wasn't keeping track of her white lies. "It's just that Jester and I have been together for so long, he's used to my cues. It will help if I can show you what I do with him."

Cindy seemed satisfied with that explanation and turned to call for a groom to take the horse away. Katie quickly reached out and loosened Jester's girth. She always let it out a couple of notches when she'd finished her ride.

"John will deliver King and his mother to your farm tomorrow. Remember, there's no trading back early, even if that colt's legs don't straighten up."

Cindy grabbed Jason's hand, dragging him toward the house. From the corner of the barn he looked back over his shoulder and waved. Katie's heart cantered in her chest. Jason Roberts had actually talked to her! Wait until she told her best friend, Jan.

⇒ Chapter Three ⇒

"They're here," her mother yelled as Katie emerged from the barn. She had gotten up at daybreak to prepare the stall for King and his mother.

The night before, old John had driven over to help Katie take down the partition in Jester's stall to make it double the size for the new arrivals. It was now bedded deep with straw and had plenty of fresh water and sweet-smelling hay. It truly was a stall fit for a king.

John maneuvered the horse trailer down the narrow driveway and parked in front of the barn that was to be King's new home. Katie hurried to help him unload the pair.

"Well, Katie girl, this is it. There's no turning back from here." John nodded hello to her mother and opened the trailer's rear doors. "Easy, easy," he crooned as the mare slowly backed out of the trailer. The colt's legs were too weak to make the twelve-inch drop to the ground, so John lifted him out.

King touched ground and surveyed his surroundings. His eyes were alert, and his ears swiveled back and forth, trying to pick up all the new sounds that surrounded him. It was a pleasant day for the middle of February in Salem, Oregon. The wind was cool, but the sun shone, illuminating King's dark brown coat and his fuzzy black mane and tail. He had just a touch of black showing on his legs now, but Katie knew that once he lost his baby hair, he would take on the true bay coloring of his father. He would be a beautiful dark bay with black points on his ears, muzzle, and legs.

King raised his head and whinnied, then struggled along after his mother, his gait slow and awkward. Katie felt as if she were watching an animal version of herself. Her heart ached with the kinship she felt with King. Come on, boy, she said to herself. It's an uphill battle, but you can do it.

"Well, Mom, what do you think?" She could tell by the skeptical look on her mother's face that she was full of doubt.

"I don't quite know what to think, dear. The poor thing can hardly walk."

"That's only temporary. He'll get stronger. You'll see." She patted her own bad leg and smiled at her mother.

They followed John and the horses into the barn. King was exhausted by the time he reached the stall. He plopped down on the soft bedding and took stock of his surroundings, then dozed off to the sound of his dam munching on hay.

"He's a pretty little thing," her mother volunteered. "But I just don't see how those legs will ever straighten out."

"Plenty of sunshine, exercise, and good food," John said.

"What do I feed him, John?"

"Nothing at present. For now, he gets all he needs from his mama."

"What about grazing? Shouldn't I be putting him out to pasture?"

"The only good pasture will do this colt is for exercising. Did you see how long his legs are? There's a reason for that. God didn't intend for a colt to be eating grass as soon as he was born. That's why their necks are so short and their legs are so long. They can't get to the grass. In a month or so, he'll start to nibbling on his mama's hay. You let me know when that happens, and we'll fix you a creep feeder."

"What's a creep feeder?" Mrs. Durham asked.

John swept off his hat and fidgeted, as if being around women made him nervous. "It's a bucket with bars over it that are spaced far enough apart so the baby can stick its nose in and eat but the mother can't. These old broodmares are a greedy bunch. They'll eat up every drop of food they can get to—even their own baby's."

John turned to Katie. "Run out to the truck and get me that bag on the seat."

Katie hurried to do his bidding. She felt fortunate to have such an experienced trainer to learn from. Mr. Ellis often said that old John had forgotten more than most trainers would ever know. He was the reason that Willow Run Farm was doing so well. She couldn't have a better teacher. She was sure that together they would see King through to fame and fortune. She grabbed the bag from the truck and returned to the barn.

"Here it is."

"That's for you, Katie girl. Go on and open it."

Katie peeked curiously into the sack. She smiled as she pulled a small halter and lead shank from the bag. "Thanks, John. When can I start using it?"

"The sooner the better. The way that colt's been eating, he'll be bigger than you pretty soon. You'd better give him some manners before then, or you'll have problems. Now is the time to handle him, while he's still weak and having trouble with his legs. Once he's got those figured out, he's going to be a handful. You mark my words."

"Do you really think there's hope for this colt?" Mrs. Durham asked the trainer.

"If they're alive, there's always hope, missus. This here colt's gotten off to a rough start in life, but I think he'll be just fine." John turned to Katie and winked. "Just be sure you take him for several walks a day for the next week or so. After that, his legs should be strong enough that he'll start exercising himself."

"But how can I walk him if he's not halter-broke?" Katie asked, disheartened. The enormousness of the project she had taken on was finally sinking in.

"Snap a lead on Grey Dancer and walk her down the shed row. He'll follow his dam. Just don't overdo it these first few days. He's weak, and we don't need him getting sick."

John unloaded the hay Mr. Ellis had sent for Grey Dancer, then left for Willow Run. Mrs. Durham returned to the house, and Katie was finally alone with her new colt. She hugged herself and laughed. She was staring at the future winner of the Portland Downs Futurity, the biggest-stakes race for two-year-olds in Oregon. And after that? Maybe she'd point him toward the Portland Derby, or even the Kentucky Derby. Who knew how far this colt could go?

King whinnied as he tried to stand and nurse, but his legs collapsed, and with them Katie's dreams. She moved into the stall and gingerly wrapped her arms around the colt's rib cage, helping him up as he tried to rise again. Shakily, he rose to his feet and made loud sucking noises, his pink tongue curling out of his mouth.

"Hold on, little guy, you're not there yet." She helped him fumble his way to his dam and smiled as he suckled greedily. "They say every race begins with the first step. We may be way behind, but we're not out of the running yet. Eat all you can, because you're going to need your strength. Tomorrow we begin your lessons."

When Katie left the barn, she headed for the back pasture, intent on seeing just how badly the fences need-ed mending. She had ridden in that field for years but had never really paid much attention to the state of the fences. No animal had been turned out there since before she could remember. The man her parents had bought this place from had raised Black Angus cattle, but Katie's family had never had more than a horse and a few chickens.

Someday, if everything went well, these fields would be full of Willow King's offspring. Maybe then they'd be able to fix up the old barn and the small house they lived in.

Katie smiled to herself. This back field was so far from the house that it was easier to keep livestock in the front pastures. But the grass was deep back there. It would be good for King to grow on.

As she trudged through the fields, she felt a niggling pain in her hip. She wished that she still had Jester. He could cover this ground in a matter of minutes. Her heart ached at the thought. She hoped Cindy would treat Jester well. If she didn't, maybe Katie could find a way to sneak him back and hide him in this pasture. She knew the plan was ridiculous, but it made her feel better all the same.

By the time she had reached her destination, her jeans were soaked to the knees. It hadn't rained since yesterday morning, but the drops were still on the grasses and plants. And now they were all on her.

She looked around the field and frowned. There were fence boards down everywhere. But at least none were missing—just fallen off the posts. This looked to be a big job. She'd better get to it today, while the sun was still out. In Oregon, you never knew when the rain would start.

Katie made her way back to the house and changed out of her wet jeans. Then she gathered up her dad's old tool belt, a hammer, and lots of nails, while her mother packed her lunch.

"Are you sure you don't need any help, honey? That sounds like a mighty big job."

"No, Mom. This is Saturday, your day off. You work

too hard as it is. I'm just going to do a little bit each day. I should be done in a couple of days."

"Have you ever nailed anything before, Katie?"

"Of course I have. I hung that picture of Grey Dancer in my bedroom. A fence post can't be much different." She didn't like the way her mother smiled at her—as though she knew something that Katie didn't. With a quick wave, she turned and headed back to the far pasture. This time, she rode her bicycle. It was easier on her joints.

Katie had her rain pants on now, so she arrived dry and comfortable. She stretched and took a deep breath of the clear, cool air. Everywhere, as far as she could see, the land was green and dotted with pines. This was a good place to grow up—for her and for Willow King.

Katie walked to the first loose board and lifted it off the wet ground. Something fuzzy skittered across her fingers, and she screamed and jumped back, throwing the board to the grass. Her heart was in her throat as she crept forward to see what sort of creepy-crawler had dared to touch her skin.

Using the hammer as a lever, she lifted the board and examined it. There was nothing there now but a couple of pill bugs. She knew they were harmless, but she knocked them off before handling the board again.

When she finally lifted the plank to the post, Katie discovered she had another problem. How was she going to keep the end of the board up while she nailed the other end?

First, she tried propping it up on another board, but it only fell off when she started to hammer. Next, she tried to hold it up by herself while she nailed it, but the weight made it tip out of her grasp when she lifted the hammer to nail. Finally, she let one end lie on the ground while she pounded a single nail into the other.

The sound of laughter startled her, and she turned to see Jason sitting atop one of his black-and-white Paints. He was only about twenty feet from her.

"You look like the Three Stooges all rolled into one."

Katie wiped the dampness from her brow and pulled a stray strand of hair away from her face. She was dirty and sweaty, and in no condition to see Jason Roberts.

And he was laughing at her.

Before she could think of what she was doing, Katie reached down and picked up a pinecone and threw it with all her might. It bounced off Jason's head and startled his horse so that it tried to jump out from under him. While he was scrambling for mane and rein, the realization of what she had just done hit her.

She had beaned Jason Roberts, megahunk of Glendale Junior High. How could she have done such a thing? If she had hurt him, she would never forgive herself. *He* would probably never forgive her.

Jason steadied his mount and reached up to rub his head. "There's no blood, so I suppose I'll live. But you're wasting your time, Katie Durham. You should be on the baseball team, not out here trying to mend fences."

For a moment Katie thought she would cry, but the smile on Jason's face stopped her. As he rode closer to the fence, she saw the pine needles in his hair, and, despite a valiant effort at keeping a serious face, she burst out laughing, the sound of her mirth spooking his horse again.

"You're a dangerous girl to be around." Jason climbed from his horse and tied him to a tree. "I came here to help you and you bean me on the head and scare my horse. I didn't know pretty girls could throw so hard."

Pretty? Did Jason just say she was pretty? She could feel the color creeping hotly up her cheeks, so she turned away from him, picking up the hammer and nails.

"Here, let me have that." He climbed over the fence and took the hammer and tool belt away from her. "I get stuck with this job at home all the time. I'm a real pro at it. Besides, things always go better with teamwork."

He winked at her, and Katie felt the butterflies take flight in her stomach.

"Stand in the middle there and hold on to this board while I nail the end. That's it," he said encouragingly.

"Why are you doing this?" Katie couldn't help but ask. None of the other boys at school would have bothered. She'd heard them snicker about limp-along Katie behind her back. It really hurt—especially since her limp wasn't that noticeable anymore. Now she was just mostly clumsy. Her heart swelled with the hope that Jason was different.

"Any friend of Cindy's is a friend of mine."

Katie's heart did a cannonball flop. Cindy. She should have known. What would a hunk like Jason want with Katie when he could have someone perfect like Cindy?

They spent the next hour repairing the fence line, then stopped for a well-earned rest. Katie shared her lunch of cold chicken and apple wedges.

"Your mom's a great cook. How about inviting me over for dinner sometime?"

Katie almost choked on her chicken leg. "Are you always so forward, Jason Roberts?"

"Are you always so shy?"

She blushed, and that was all the answer he got. They finished the rest of their lunch in silence. Katie could feel every bite she took stick in her throat.

They went back to work, and to her surprise they were done with the entire project in another hour. Her spirits picked up, and she forgot about her earlier disappointment. "This is great!" Katie exclaimed. "I thought it would take me a week."

"The way you were going, it would have taken you at least a month."

"Watch it, mister. I've got a never-ending supply of pinecones at my disposal," she teased as she hefted one in her hand.

Jason threw his arms up as if to protect himself. "Anything but that."

"No, really, how can I ever thank you? You saved me a lot of work, not to mention the headache."

"I told you–invite me to dinner. My mom's away for two weeks, and my dad's doing the cooking. I think I've lost five pounds since she left."

"I'm not sure if my mother is up to entertaining. She works really hard, and she's always tired when she gets home at night." Katie hoped that would discourage him.

35

She wouldn't be able to eat a bite with Jason sitting at her table.

"I'll take a rain check for now." He smiled. "I think we're eating out tonight. I can survive that. You be good and keep working on that right arm. I'm going to have a talk with the baseball coach come Monday."

Katie smiled. He knew she'd be lousy at running bases with her bum leg, but it was nice of him to act as if it didn't matter.

With a smile and a wink, Jason mounted his horse and was gone, leaving her to think that maybe she had imagined the whole thing. She looked at the repaired fence, and a smile came to her lips. Jason hadn't taken her out, bought her dinner, or even a Coke, but she'd just worked like a teammate with the boy of her dreams.

☞ Chapter Four ☜

Katie woke often during the night to check the new foal. The first days and nights of his life were extremely important. If he didn't get all the nourishment he needed, he would die.

She found King lying listlessly on the straw. The short trip from Willow Run Farm to his new home had exhausted him, and he had trouble standing on his own. Trying to get him up to nurse was a real chore. Katie had to stretch his legs in front of his body and prop him up so he was sitting like a dog, then run around and lift his hindquarters. More often than not, when his back half came off the ground, the front would collapse.

Jason was right: she felt as if she were in a Three Stooges movie.

Once King was up and nursing, Katie wrapped her arms around him to steady him. He leaned heavily on her, and at times she felt her arms were ready to drop off. But the colt got a full meal each time, and she could see he was gaining strength by the hour.

Katie was glad it wasn't a school night, because she was losing energy as rapidly as King was gaining it. And her hip pained her something awful. She wondered if King's legs hurt. Why couldn't she have raised parakeets or puppies? It would have been so much easier. A horse was a big responsibility, but a problem horse was even more so.

She stroked King's soft coat. Newborn foals felt like velvet. She ran her hand over the colt's malformed legs, marveling at their delicate structure. Was it crazy for her to believe that someday these twisted limbs would straighten and become the solid bone and muscle of a running machine?

Yet, she did believe it.

Katie had enough faith to make up for all the doubters. She knew King would be a champion one day. But right now, seeing him so weak and helpless in the straw, that day seemed a long way off.

She touched his little legs again. "I hope these don't pain you as much as my legs pain me." Katie sighed. "You've got to pull through this, King," she pleaded as she ruffled his wispy mane. "If we lose you, we lose it all—you, Jester, the farm. You've got to get stronger, boy. We've got some good times ahead of us and lots of winner's circles to pose in."

She moved to the corner of the stall where the straw was deep and clean, and sat down to rest, tucking her hands into the pockets of her warm jacket. As her eyelids grew heavy, she snuggled further into her coat and the straw.

*   *   *

Katie woke when the farm's rooster, Chicken George, crowed his wake-up call. The weak rays of the early morning sun filtered through the cracks in the old barn, giving everything a dreamworld appearance.

She sat up and rubbed her eyes, wondering how far past King's mealtime she had slept. When she looked about, she saw he was standing and nursing on his own. His legs were wobbling, but they managed to hold him upright. She wanted to jump up and shout for joy, but that would startle the colt. And, sore as she was from sleeping on the barn floor, she doubted she would be able to jump.

Katie waited until he was done, then slipped quietly out of the stall and back to her bedroom. As she tiptoed down the hall, her mother poked her head out of her room.

"How's the colt?"

"He's finally eating on his own."

"Good. Now you can get some sleep. I'll check on the colt and call you if anything goes wrong. Good night, dear."

"Good night, Mom. Oh, and Mom?"

Mrs. Durham looked into her daughter's tired but happy eyes. "Yes, honey?"

"You're the greatest. Thanks for understanding." She gave her mother a hug, then disappeared into her room.

It was mid-afternoon when Katie finally opened her eyes. She jumped out of bed and scrambled into her clothing, tripping and almost falling when her foot got caught in a pant leg.

"Hey, sleepyhead," her mother called as she entered the kitchen.

"How's the colt?" Katie tried to keep the rising panic out of her voice, but her mother knew her too well.

Mrs. Durham wrapped her arms around Katie's shoulders and gave her a peck on the cheek. "Everything's great, honey. I've checked on him every hour, and each time I go out there, he's eating. I don't know if he keeps getting up to eat again, or if he never stops."

Katie breathed a sigh of relief and hugged her mother. "Thanks, Mom. It's you, me, and King against the world. Nobody else thinks this colt will make it."

Mrs. Durham reached out and stroked her daughter's hair. "I hate to burst your bubble, but I've still got my doubts."

"I know you do, Mom, but you'll come around. Until then, I've got enough faith for both of us."

Katie grabbed a piece of toast, then ran out the door to the barn. Just as her mother had said, King was up and nursing, his little mop of a tail flicking happily. Grey Dancer nickered a greeting, and King paused to inspect the intruder who had interrupted his meal. With a flip of his head, he dismissed her and went back to his lunch.

"You're not going to ignore me that easily." Katie laughed as she pulled the halter off its hook. She entered the stall and walked up to the colt, dangling it in front of him. "It's lesson time."

She quickly slipped the halter on and fastened it. King bobbed his head several times to dislodge it. When it wouldn't budge, he accepted it and went back to nursing.

"Wow, I hope everything goes this smoothly with you."

Katie ran her hands over the colt's body, getting him used to her touch. A ticklish horse was difficult to handle. John said a colt should be worked with as soon as it stood to nurse.

King stomped his feet and tried to wiggle out of her grasp, but Katie continued fondling his ears and running a hand down his legs. Despite his weakened condition, he fought the lesson, and they went around and around the stall. King flopped around like a freshly caught fish, but Katie refused to let him go. By the time the colt finally relented, Katie was drenched in sweat and King was ready to drop. His nostrils flared and his chest heaved.

"So much for smooth going," Katie muttered as she removed the halter and collapsed in the corner. For the hundredth time, she asked herself what she had gotten into. This was supposed to be simple: raise a colt, get him to the racetrack, win lots of races. She had never raised a foal before, and she was beginning to suspect that there was plenty she didn't know.

The next several lessons went the same way. Katie started to doubt the wisdom of her decision. King was as stubborn as a mule. Five days passed, and still she hadn't been able to take him for the walks that John had suggested. King was so worn out after their battles, that he collapsed in the straw and slept for hours afterward. But he was definitely getting stronger. Her aching arms were proof of that.

She was getting stronger too—mentally, as well as

physically. All her life people had told her she couldn't do things because of her slight disability. She knew she had her limitations; who didn't? But she was tired of people thinking she couldn't perform. She looked down at her sneakers. They were a matched set—not her special pair. So what if she limped a little? She could do most things every bit as good as the rest of the kids in her class, and some things even better. King was going to be one of those things. Together, they would soar to the top!

The following day, Katie decided to give the colt a break. She didn't want to admit that she needed one too, but the soreness of her muscles every time she moved was a constant nagging reminder.

King was now moving around the stall in a slow, shuffling gait. Walking didn't seem to be such a chore anymore. Tomorrow she would take him and his dam for a walk down the shed row.

When Katie entered the stall, King ambled over and poked her with his nose. Katie reached out to pet him, then stayed her hand, not wanting to start another battle. She picked up the brushes and ran them over Grey Dancer's slick coat. Soon she heard a rustling of straw, and King stuck his head around his mother's tail. After another moment, he came to stand beside Katie, nibbling at her shirttails.

"You think you want some brushing too?" Katie asked as she stroked him with the brush, expecting him to shy away. But the colt stood quietly, his little fox ears flicking back and forth and his tail swishing when she hit a ticklish spot. "Well, I'll be." She moved the grooming tool over his entire body, even under his belly, and still the colt didn't budge.

Katie replaced the brush strokes with her hands, moving them down his front legs, then back up and over his hindquarters. She didn't know whether to be happy or mad. After all their skirmishes, all the doubts and bruises, here he stood as if nothing were amiss.

Looking at the unpredictable colt, who continued to nibble at her clothing, she knew she couldn't stay mad at him. Getting angry didn't seem to do any good anyway. He definitely had a stubborn streak.

For the next several days, Katie took King and his mother for short walks. His legs were just as crooked as ever, but he was rapidly gaining in strength. It was time to break him to halter and lead.

After school the next day, Katie led Grey Dancer out of the stall and tied her in the shed row. She got King's halter off the hook and put it on him, but this time she left the lead rope attached. He had been so good the past week that she counted on an easy lesson.

Once again, the colt proved her wrong.

Katie gently pulled on the lead rope. King balked and pulled back. She tugged a little harder, and he quickly backed up, hitting the barn wall behind him, then lunging away from her. Katie kept hold of the rope and was dragged off her feet, hitting the ground face-down and bouncing along the hard dirt floor.

She got to her feet, spitting dirt and brushing the straw out of her hair, when she heard an amused chuckle coming from the doorway. She turned to see Jason astride his large Paint horse just outside the barn.

"It looks like the Three Stooges are at it again. Only I guess I would have to call you guys the Two Stooges since it doesn't look like the gray mare is involved."

"What are you doing here?" Katie frowned as she brushed more pieces of debris from her jeans. Why did he have to show up now?

"I thought I would stop by and see how the colt was doing. It looks like he's feeling his oats," Jason said with a smile.

Katie wanted to slap that silly grin right off his face. What a sight she must be! Dirt stains covered her clothing from head to toe, and her hair was a tangled mess of straw and pieces of alfalfa. She stood in the middle of the shed row, biting her lip and willing herself not to cry. Why did these things always happen to her? Well, they didn't *always* happen, she just seemed to be more awkward since Jason decided to step out of her dreams and into her life. And why was she always so clumsy? She looked down at her bad leg and frowned.

Jason was a puzzle too. The real-life boy didn't jibe with the one in her fantasy. Oh, sure, he was just as handsome, and he had an awesome personality, but that's where the similarities ended. In her dreamworld she had on her best clothes and her hair was always perfect. She never said or did anything that wasn't just right—and she didn't walk with a limp. And, of course, Jason thought she was beautiful and witty. He was charming as a prince, and he made her feel special.

Right now, all she felt was embarrassed and angry.

Jason dismounted and led his horse into an empty stall, pulling the saddle and bridle off and throwing them over the door.

"What are you doing?" She coiled her lead shank, and King walked up to her, sticking his nose into her hair and blowing a warm breath across her cheeks.

"See, he's trying to apologize to you."

Katie stood in the center of the barn. She reached out to stroke the colt's neck, refusing to look at Jason.

"I guess I owe you an apology, too. I'm sorry, Katie. I wasn't trying to make fun of you. It's just that...well, you did look awfully funny sweeping the barn floor with the front of your shirt."

In her mind's eye, Katie could see the incident just as Jason described it. She could feel a small grin tugging at the corners of her mouth. After one look at the twinkle in Jason's eyes, she burst out laughing. It wasn't funny— but, then again, it was.

"That's much better. Am I safe coming around you now, or do you have a stash of pinecones somewhere?"

"No, you're safe. But you still didn't answer my question. Why did you untack your horse?" She ran her hand through King's unruly mane and glanced at Jason out of the corner of her eye.

He stopped beside her and reached out to pluck a few stems of hay from her hair. "You look like you could use some help."

"I'm doing just fine, Jason Roberts," Katie huffed. "You can resaddle your horse and ride on out of here. I don't need any help."

Jason said nothing. He just stood there and stared at

her with those heavenly blue eyes. She wished he would look away. He made her feel ashamed of herself for acting like such a child.

"Well, maybe I *could* use a little help," she relented, then shrugged her shoulders and looked him straight in the eye. "The truth is, I need a lot of it. I've never raised a colt before, and I think I'm doing it all wrong. Every time I pull him to come forward, he puts it in reverse."

Jason smiled and stepped up to take the lead from her hand. "Don't worry about that. It's a pretty natural reaction from a colt. I've helped my dad raise lots of them, and none of the colts ever got it right the first time. It takes a lot of work."

"I'm beginning to understand just how much work this really is. I didn't think it would be this hard." She inspected the scrapes on her palms.

"Some are more difficult than others. You've just got to have patience."

"So where do we start?" Katie asked.

Jason threw the rope over King's back and went to untie Grey Dancer. "First, we get him back in the stall with his mama."

"But there's hardly any room in there."

"That's the idea." Jason flashed her a winsome smile. "There will be less room for him to drag you around."

Katie made a face at him.

"I'm not joking, girl. Pulling back is a natural response for these colts. King already weighs as much as you do, and he's got four legs to pull with. He's going to win every time. The trick is to convince him that he wants to do what *you* want."

Katie held the stall door open until the mare and foal entered, then she and Jason stepped inside and closed the door. "How do we do that? He's almost convinced me that I should let him do what *he* wants. He's very determined."

Jason laughed. "That's what it takes to make a good runner. Once he learns how to channel that stubbornness into his racing, he'll be hard to beat."

Katie brightened. Jason talked as though the colt would make it. She'd been having her doubts, but he was giving her the encouragement that she needed to continue. "Let's get started."

Jason grabbed the colt by the halter and placed his other hand on his hindquarters. "You want to start by turning him in circles. Teach him to follow his nose." He gave a slight tug on the colt's head and a gentle push on his hips, and King made an awkward turn to the left. "See? At first he'll step more readily to the side than forward." Jason switched and turned the colt in the other direction.

"Wow!" Katie clapped her hands. "Can I try?"

Jason stood behind her and positioned her hands on the halter and the colt's rump. Standing this close to Jason with his hands covering hers, she was a nervous wreck. She tried to concentrate on the task, hoping he couldn't feel her shake. King tried to put up a fight, but with his head being pulled to the side, he was off balance and forced to make the turn.

"Now pet him and tell him what a good boy he is," Jason instructed.

While Katie was rewarding King, Jason took a long

rope down from the wall and tied it into a lasso.

"You're not going to rope him, are you?"

"No, this is for helping him to learn how to walk forward." He placed the rope so it encircled the colt's hindquarters. "When you pull on the halter and he doesn't come, just give a tug on the butt rope and the colt will think he's being pushed from behind."

Katie tried it, and King took a few tentative steps toward her. Soon she was leading him around the stall. "You're a lifesaver, Jason. How can I ever thank you? You've saved me a lot of headaches."

"What about that dinner invitation?"

When he stared at her with those clear blue eyes, she couldn't think straight. She had to wiggle out of this one. There was no way she could eat with him sitting at the same table. "Uh, I can't tonight. My friend Jan is coming over for dinner, and it wouldn't be fair to my mom to have to prepare for another person on such a short notice." She shrugged her shoulders. "It's too late—dinner's almost ready. Sorry."

"Katie?" her mother called as she stepped through the barn door. "Jan is here." She stopped when she saw Katie had company. "Why, Jason, look at you. You're all grown up! I haven't seen you in quite a while. How are your parents?"

"Just fine, Mrs. Durham. It's nice to see you again."

"Katie, how come you never invite Jason over? I went to school with his mother. We just seem to have lost touch over the years. It's good to see that you two are picking up the friendship."

Katie stared at her mother with her mouth agape,

trying to think of something logical to say. Obviously, her mom didn't notice her loss for words because she just kept on talking.

"Would you like to stay for dinner tonight, Jason? We've got plenty to go around."

Jason's back was to Katie, so she raised her hands, making a no-go motion in the air and violently shaking her head. She quickly put her hands behind her back when he turned to smile at her.

"I would love to join you ladies for dinner. Can I use your phone to call my dad and make sure it's okay?"

"Right this way, dear." Mrs. Durham turned in the doorway to look back at Katie. "Are you feeling all right, honey? You look a little pale."

"No, Mom, everything's fine," she said, though she was dying to shout out her frustration. She hugged herself, trying to calm her rolling stomach. What was she going to do now? Jason Roberts was coming to dinner!

⊶ Chapter Five ⊷

Katie pushed the food around on her plate. Lasagna was one of her favorite dishes, but she just couldn't work up an appetite. Fortunately, her mother carried most of the conversation. Katie couldn't think of anything to say, and all Jan did was sit there with a goofy look on her face and smile.

Katie stretched her foot under the table and kicked her friend in the shin. "Stop staring," she mouthed. Jan's answer was a return kick, and Jan went back to watching Jason.

How did she get herself into these things? This was one of those situations that her mother would say she would laugh at when she was older. Maybe eons from now, after the mountains had turned to dust and risen again, but not now.

"Isn't that right, Katie?" Mrs. Durham asked and Katie's head popped up like a jack-in-the-box.

"I'm sorry, Mom. I didn't hear what you said." All eyes were on her. She could feel the color rising in her cheeks.

"I was just telling Jason that you have high hopes for Willow King."

Now she was going to be forced to speak. She tried for a smile and hoped it didn't look too sickly. "That's right" was all she could manage to say.

"Honey, do you feel all right? You're usually quite the chatterbox. I hope you're not getting the flu."

Katie groaned inwardly. Jason knew she felt just fine. He would attribute her bashful silence to himself–and would probably enjoy it. Well, she wouldn't give him the satisfaction. "No, Mom. I'm just a little tired. King and I had a rough day today." She glared at Jason, daring him to say one word about her trip down the shed row on her stomach.

Jason winked at her and helped himself to another serving of lasagna. "If that colt's legs ever straighten out, he should be one heck of a racehorse. He's got the body of a runner: large hindquarters, deep chest, long legs, and lots of size."

Katie grew defensive. "His legs *will* straighten out. You'll see. John says that after a summer of running on pasture, he'll be a whole new horse. John hasn't been wrong about too many things." She spoke confidently, then said a quick prayer that this wouldn't be one of his mistakes. It couldn't be. King had to make it.

"You're lucky to be able to work with John. My father says he's one of the best trainers around. He's from the old school."

"What do you mean by that?" Jan finally joined the conversation.

Jason picked up the salad bowl and forked some

51

lettuce onto his plate. "My dad says these new trainers are in too much of a hurry to get their horses to the track. They run the legs off them with short, quick workouts, and the horses usually have leg trouble by the time they get to the races. Instead of giving them time off, the trainers patch them up—or drug them so they can't feel the pain—and run them anyway."

"But isn't that illegal?" Katie was horrified that something like that could happen.

"Not all drugs are illegal. Lasix and bute are allowed at many tracks around the country, including Portland Downs."

"What are Lasix and bute?" Katie was surprised that Jason knew so much about racehorses.

"Sometimes after a hard race, horses will bleed a little from the lungs or nostril lining. You'll notice a small amount of blood coming out of their nostrils. You can put them on Lasix, and most of the time they won't bleed again. If they do, they're ruled off and can't run anywhere. Bute is short for some fancy medical name. All you have to remember is that it's like a big aspirin. It gets rid of their aches and pains. Of course, in Oregon it's illegal to run a horse on either of these drugs unless the track veterinarian examines the horse and gives you permission."

Katie looked at Jason with admiration. What a waste that he was going with a no-brain like Cindy Ellis.

"Why would someone run an injured horse?" Jan inquired.

"For the money," Katie answered. "I've heard John complain about people who abuse their horses for the sake of a paycheck."

"Are you sure you want to go into this business, Katie?" Jan asked.

"It's not all that bad," Jason offered. "Most people treat their horses very well. A racehorse is a big investment, and most of them are pampered. It's just that a few bad people always manage to spoil things and give the sport a bad name."

"I'll never let that happen to King," Katie vowed.

The rest of the dinner was occupied with small talk, and finally Jason pushed back from the table and rose to leave.

"Thanks for the great meal, Mrs. Durham. You've saved me from another night of TV dinners. With my mom gone for another week, that's about all my dad can cook." He peered out the window. "The sun's starting to go down and I've got to get my horse home before dark." He nodded to Katie and Jan, then reached for his jacket.

"Katie, dear, why don't you see your friend to the door while Jan and I clean up the dishes? Jason, it was so good to see you again. Tell your folks I said hello, and come back and see us again real soon. Katie talks about you, but she never invites you over. Feel free to drop in anytime."

"Thank you, I'll do that." He turned and looked at Katie with a knowing grin.

Katie about died on the spot. Why did her mother have to tell him that she talked about him? All she ever told her mother was how helpful and encouraging Jason had been lately. Now he would think that she had a crush on him. She looked to Jan, whose eyes were popping out of her head so far you could have knocked them off with a stick, but Jan wasn't any help.

Katie couldn't get the door open fast enough. Jason said his good-byes, and she practically slammed the door on his heels. Then she leaned against the wood and closed her eyes. She had acted like a spineless coward all during the meal. And now, thanks to her mother, Jason would think that she had a big crush on him. She would never be able to look him in the eye again. Life was so unfair.

"I can't believe I sat at a table with Jason Roberts!" Jan squealed when she and Katie were alone in Katie's room. "He was right there before my very eyes. Did you notice he likes Thousand Island dressing on his salad?" Jan was totally enthralled.

"Did you notice what a fool I made of myself!" Katie cried. Who cared what he ate on his salad? Her life was going down the tubes. By Monday, it would be all over school that she had a crush on Jason. How could her mother have done such a thing?

Katie sighed. It really wasn't her mom's fault. After all, she didn't bring many of her school friends home. It was just bad luck that things turned out the way they had. There seemed to be a lot of that going around lately.

"I think he likes you," Jan said. "You're so lucky. I wish it were me."

"Don't be dense. Jason doesn't like me—he's already got a girlfriend."

"Who?"

"Cindy Ellis." Katie sat down cross-legged on the bed and picked up a stuffed bear, hugging it closely to her. "She doesn't deserve a guy like him."

"Cindy Ellis? But she's an underclassman. He could have any girl in the whole school. Why would he pick her?"

Katie punched her pillow and leaned back against the headboard. "Why *wouldn't* he pick her? She's beautiful, graceful, she wears nice clothes, hangs out with all the popular kids, and her dad owns one of the biggest Thoroughbred ranches in Salem. And in case you hadn't noticed it, *we* are underclassmen, and you seem to think Jason likes me. Of course he would go for Cindy."

"But you're not stuck-up like Cindy. And besides, if I can't have him, it might as well be my best friend who gets him. How do you know he's Cindy's boyfriend? I've never seen them together at school. Did he tell you that?"

"No, Cindy told me, and I saw it with my own eyes. He was at Willow Run the day I took Jester there."

"Being there doesn't make him her boyfriend, you know."

"I saw them holding hands."

Jan chewed at her bottom lip, clearly not believing the information she was hearing. "You can say what you want, Katie, but I don't think he's got a thing for Cindy. I think he's got his eye on you."

"Yeah, right. Jason likes my mother's cooking, and that's about it. And after everything that's happened this week, he probably thinks I'm a real klutz."

"What happened this week? We're best buddies, remember? You're supposed to tell me everything." Jan sat forward, eager to hear the latest news.

"I'm sorry, I was going to phone you, but between taking care of the colt and doing some grooming at the Ellis place, I've been so busy I haven't had time to sit down. And since we don't have any classes together this year and you've got second lunch...." Katie shrugged her shoulders.

"Okay, I forgive you. Just give me the latest scoop."

Katie pulled up another pillow and stretched out on the bed. Jan did the same.

"The first time I ever spoke to Jason was just after King was born. I rode Jester over to give him to Cindy, and Jason was there."

"Doesn't that kill you to see her riding your horse? That girl couldn't ride the Greyhound bus without a seat belt!"

They had a good laugh, and Mrs. Durham poked her head into the room. "What's all the giggling about? Sounds like you're talking about boys. I'm sure I know who the center of the conversation is."

"Oh, Mom."

"Don't be embarrassed, honey. He's a very nice boy. I'm glad you finally brought him over." She set a couple of glasses of soda on the nightstand. "I'll go now and leave you girls to your talk."

Katie waited until the door closed before she continued. "After John brought King here, I went out to the back pasture to check the fence."

"What are you doing with the back pasture? You've got plenty of good paddocks around the house."

"Mr. Ellis doesn't want this colt anywhere that he can be seen. That's part of the deal. He's afraid someone will recognize Grey Dancer with King and start asking questions. He doesn't want anybody to find out his stud threw a crooked-legged foal."

"Hmph!" Jan snorted. "He'll be sorry he gave this colt up when he wins all the big races."

"My feelings exactly. Anyway, so I'm out in this pasture trying to nail up boards, and guess who happens by?"

Jan sat up and drew her arms around her legs. "Jason?"

"You got it. I was having a hard time, and he started laughing at me, so I picked up a pinecone and chucked it at him."

"You didn't!"

"Yes, I did. I bounced it off the top of his head. I still can't believe I did it. I was so embarrassed."

"It's a good thing you didn't mark up that gorgeous face, or all the girls at Glendale would run you out of town."

"He helped me with the fence and asked if I would invite him over for dinner sometime. I didn't see him again until today. This time, when he walked in the barn, I was taking a ride down the shed row on my belly. I tell you, Jan, I just can't seem to do anything right around the guy. How could he like somebody like me? I feel like such an ugly duckling when I'm around

Cindy. She's so popular and pretty. She always wears the latest styles, and she never has a hair out of place. How can I compete with that? Especially with this," she said as she touched her bad leg.

Jan patted her shoulder. "Don't be so hard on yourself, pal. How could he not like you? You've got everything over that dumb ol' Cindy Ellis. You've got a natural beauty—you don't need tons of makeup and new hairstyles to look good. And when it comes to horses, Cindy is like a parakeet with its wings clipped, and you soar like an eagle. If he chooses her over you, then I say let them have each other. Anybody with that much bad taste isn't worth having—no matter how gorgeous he is."

They finished their sodas, and Jan went home. Katie made one last check on the colt and settled in for the night.

The next morning, Katie got up early and spent some time brushing Willow King before she set out for Willow Run Farm. "I'll be back later and we can go for a nice walk," she promised King as she threw the currycomb into the brush box and exited the stall.

In keeping with her agreement, she was to spend at least two hours a day, three days a week, helping around the Ellis farm. Katie was glad of the opportunity. There was a lot she needed to learn about racehorses. Things she hadn't paid much attention to before were now vitally important.

Her responsibilities at the farm included holding a horse for the groom to tack. Then, while the horse was out for his run, Katie cleaned the stall and put in fresh feed and bedding. This had to be finished by the time the horse returned so she could be ready to help with the washing and cooling of the animal.

A Thoroughbred was never put back in his stall until he was completely cooled down from his workout. Willow Run Farm had several automatic hot-walkers. These were large metal machines with a central pole and four arms to which the horses' halters were hooked. The arms rotated, walking the horses in a circle, cooling them off after their run.

Every few minutes Katie would stop the hot-walker and give the horses a small sip of water. John cautioned her against giving them too much at once. If a horse was excessively hot and drank a lot, he could get colic and become extremely ill.

Katie didn't want to risk inflicting that torture on one of the high-strung beauties, but it was difficult to ignore the whinnies and pleading looks when she stopped the walker. The hotter the horse was, the deeper he thrust his muzzle into the bucket, and the harder it was to take the pail away. But Katie knew she had to for the horse's sake.

Even though these were large, powerful animals, they were very delicate and often did things that were potentially dangerous.

It was exciting working with these kings of the wind, and she loved every minute of it. Someday she would be doing this for her own horse. While she busied herself with cleaning, her imagination ran amuck. In her daydreams, Willow King claimed victory after victory, and always, she and Jester were there to escort him to the winner's circle.

A loud commotion drew Katie out of her fantasy world, and she ran into the barn's shed row to see what was happening. "Stupid horse!" Cindy was shouting as she rode Jester down the barn aisle and past a half-dozen stalls, scattering grooms and game hens alike. Cindy sawed on the bit, turning the horse this way and that while she beat him with a riding crop.

Jester danced along the pathway, throwing his head and rolling his eyes. Never, in all the years that she had owned him, had Katie ever seen him behave this way. He was out of control, and Cindy was of no more use than a mouse at the switch of a runaway train.

Katie ran toward them, waving her arms in the air. She prayed that Jester would recognize her and not mow her down. "Whoa, whoa!" she yelled as the horse drew nearer.

Jester planted all four legs and slid to a halt in front of her, almost unseating his young rider. As bad an equestrian as Cindy was, Katie was surprised that she managed to stay on. The horse's sides were heaving, and he stamped his feet, snorting nervously.

"What's going on in here?" Mr. Ellis charged into the barn like a raging bull.

"Nothing, Daddy." Cindy looked at Katie, daring her to refute her words.

"What do you mean *nothing?* I've had two grooms come to me saying that you're running up and down the barn with this horse. You know I don't allow that."

Knowing she had been caught, Cindy tried a different approach.

"I'm sorry, Father, but this horse is being a real jerk today. He won't listen to a thing I say." She moved the crop to the other side of the saddle so her dad wouldn't see it.

"I know this horse, young lady. He's a perfectly behaved animal, or I wouldn't have let you have him."

Tom Ellis approached the gelding and noted his agitated state. "What's this?" He put his hand to Jester's side, and it came away red with blood. He grabbed the spur on Cindy's boot and wrenched it off her ankle. "Don't you have any more sense than to ride a well-mannered horse with spurs? No wonder he's a wreck. Get down off his back until he's calmed down."

Mr. Ellis turned to Katie. "I'm sorry you had to see this. Sometimes Cindy doesn't have a lick of sense." He turned to his daughter. "Katie's going to calm this horse down, then you and she are going out to that arena, and you are going to take some lessons from her. If you can't get this horse under control and learn how to ride him properly, then we'll just have to give him back to Katie." He turned on his heel and walked away, leaving Cindy to sulk and glare at his retreating form.

Katie stood rooted to the spot. Would he really give Jester back to her? It was a wonderful thought. All she had to do was give Cindy the wrong cues—not that she needed any help in that department—and Jester would soon be back in her barn.

She looked at the horse and her heart gave a lurch. In the ten days that Jester had been here, he had changed a lot. His coat wasn't as shiny, and he had lost some weight. How much more of this mistreatment could he take before he finally flipped his lid and became a rank horse?

She couldn't take that chance. Not with Jester. He meant the world to her, and his happiness, whether it was in Cindy's hands or her own, was very important. She would swallow her selfish desires and teach Cindy how to handle him properly.

⇒ Chapter Six ⇒

Mr. Ellis had handed Jester's reins to Katie, but as soon as he turned the corner of the barn, Cindy snatched them out of Katie's hands and glared at her.

"Don't think that you can teach me anything, Katie Durham. You're a kid, just like I am. I don't have to do anything you say. I'm going along with this because my father is really mad, and I know he'll be watching. You can't ride any better than I can. The only reason you beat me at the shows is because the judges around here have a soft spot for underdogs." She looked pointedly at Katie's corrective shoe. "They don't like me because my dad is rich." She glanced at Katie's clothing and curled her lips in distaste. "You don't even dress like a proper horsewoman."

Katie flinched at the meanness in her tone. She looked down at her baggy sweatpants and old windbreaker. It was true, she wasn't exactly a fashion plate. Not that she was sloppy. Her school clothes were always clean and pressed, and the riding jacket and breeches she used for shows were always in good repair. Her mother just didn't have the money to buy the designer brands that Cindy wore. And a lot of good they did her. Cindy still couldn't win in her classes.

She looked at Cindy, noting the red splotches that stained her cheeks and the way she squinted her eyes. And to think that only a few days ago Cindy had been talking about what great friends they were going to be. But that was back when she was getting her way. Things weren't going so smoothly now.

Katie had heard the kids at school talk about Cindy's temper tantrums. She'd even seen a few of the minor ones, but never had Katie been on the receiving end of such intense hostility. She didn't like it one bit, but she was in a precarious position. She needed her job at Willow Run to help pay for King's expenses. If she opened her mouth and told Cindy what she thought, it might jeopardize her job.

Katie bit back the retort that was on her tongue. Clothes didn't make a person. And she couldn't help her handicap; that would be with her for life. But even with that small setback, she knew she was a better rider than Cindy—and so did the judges. The brat was just blowing off steam, and she didn't care who got hurt in the process. As long as Katie knew the truth, she couldn't worry about what was said by a nasty, spiteful, jealous girl.

Cindy would get her comeuppance in the ring this summer. Jester was a great competitor, but he couldn't do it all himself. If Cindy didn't learn how to handle him, she was in for another ribbonless season.

When Katie didn't say a word, Cindy snorted disdainfully and turned on her heel, pulling hard on Jester's reins. The horse's head popped up at the sudden pressure on his mouth. He snorted in protest before following reluctantly behind her. "Let's get this over with. I have better things to do with my time," Cindy said. "There's a dance next Saturday, and I want Jason to take me to it. I've got to find a new outfit to wear. I never see you at the dances. I guess it's hard to find a partner when you're clumsy."

That hurt. Katie stared furiously at the back of Cindy's head. She wore her new breeches and an expensive pair of riding boots. She stomped away with her nose pointed toward the sky. How Jason Roberts ever got mixed up with the likes of her, Katie would never know. She couldn't picture the two of them together. They said that love was blind, but in his case it was blind, deaf, and dumb.

When they reached the arena, Katie followed Cindy inside and closed the gate. She wasn't sure what to do. She knew that Cindy didn't want her help, but she also knew that Mr. Ellis expected her to make an improvement in his daughter's riding ability. Nothing like asking for the impossible, Katie thought. But anything would be an improvement over what Cindy was doing now. If she could just get Cindy to listen to her, she knew she could help. And she knew she had to try for Jester's sake.

"I guess I better get on my horse and make it look like we're doing something," Cindy said as she gathered her reins and inserted her left foot into the stirrup of the English saddle. She put all her weight into the iron, preparing to swing up, when the saddle slipped, ending sideways on Jester's rib cage.

Katie sucked in her breath as she watched the girl fall to the ground beneath the horse's feet, her foot still caught in the stirrup. Cindy shrieked like a banshee and thrashed about, trying to free herself. Katie came to her senses and quickly stepped forward calling, "Whoa, whoa," to Jester as she approached.

Fortunately, Jester was a fairly calm horse, and all he did was side pass, crossing one leg over the other, traveling sideways to try to escape his squawking rider.

"Cindy, be quiet!" Katie hissed under her breath as she reached out for the horse's rein. Jester stood quietly for her while a furious, sand-covered Cindy freed her foot from the iron.

Cindy got to her feet, brushing the sand from her clothing in quick, angry strokes, then reached up to tuck the loose ends of hair back into her French braid. "I suppose you think this is hilarious?" She glared at Katie. "If you tell anyone at school about this, you'll be sorry."

If it wasn't such a dangerous situation, Katie might have laughed to see the high and mighty Cindy Ellis brought down a peg or two, but it wasn't a laughing matter. Katie undid the girth and let the saddle fall to the ground. It landed with a thump.

"I didn't think it was funny at all. You could have been seriously hurt." She turned to Cindy as she shook the sand from the saddle blanket. "That's why you should never ride when you're upset. Riding requires a person's full attention. When you've got other stuff on your mind, you forget to do important things like check your equipment, and you can end up hurt."

Sparks flew from Cindy's green eyes as she stared at

Katie, but this time Katie stood her ground. In the next instant the fire went out, and Cindy hung her head and started to shake. It seemed that the realization of what could have happened just hit her.

"It's okay." Katie stepped forward and awkwardly patted Cindy's shoulder. She felt funny seeing the snobbish Miss Ellis caught in a vulnerable moment. "We all make mistakes. As long as you're not hurt and you learn from it, you'll be okay."

Cindy's blond head snapped up and her proud manner returned. "That's easy for you to say. You weren't the one being trampled beneath the hooves of a crazed animal."

Katie looked at Jester as he stood patiently waiting for them to resaddle him. He was a little wary, but he didn't look like a dangerous beast. She replaced the saddle blanket, then settled the saddle back into place, taking care to ensure the girth was properly tightened.

Katie ran a hand over the spur marks Cindy had caused. They had stopped bleeding and weren't as bad as she had originally thought, but they would need medication. She would drop by Jester's stall after Cindy was gone, and tend to the wounds. She turned her attention back to Cindy.

"Oh, I've been dumped plenty of times," Katie assured the shaken girl. "I've been bucked off, knocked off, just plain fallen off, and pushed down when I wasn't even intending to ride the horse. You have to remember what you did wrong and learn from your mistakes."

When she finished checking all the equipment, she turned to Cindy, who was looking at her skeptically.

"What are you doing?" the girl asked nervously. "Shouldn't we put Jester back in his stall and let him calm down?"

Katie ran a hand down the horse's neck. "He's all right. You won't have any problems with him now. I think we'd better work on mounting. You've got to learn how to distribute your weight so you don't pull the saddle over on the horse's side. Did you know that at the famous riding school in Vienna they teach the riders to mount without a girth on their saddle? There's nothing to hold the saddle in place, yet they can put their foot in the stirrup and mount up without disturbing the placement of the saddle."

"I think you're telling me a tall tale, Katie Durham. I don't believe anybody can do that."

"No, really, it's the truth. I can't do it, but it's something to shoot for. Now, pay attention. This is what I want you to do." She picked up the reins and placed her left hand on the crest of the horse's neck, just in front of the saddle, and her right hand on the pommel at the front of the saddle.

"Put your hands like this," she instructed. "If you have trouble at first, you can grip the saddle. Place your left foot in the iron and think of shooting your weight up into the saddle. Never try to push all your weight downward, or you'll pull the saddle over to the side if it's loose. Vault yourself up, then swing your right leg over the horse."

She demonstrated the move with fluid motion, then quickly dismounted. "Your turn." She handed the reins to Cindy.

The girl just stood there fumbling with the reins. "I don't think this is such a good idea. Maybe we should wait till tomorrow. I think it will be a lot better then." She started to walk Jester back to the barn.

"Wait!" Katie ran to block their exit. She couldn't let Cindy leave without making her get back on the horse. The fall had unnerved Cindy, and now she was afraid to remount. When Katie started riding, the same thing had happened to her. If her father hadn't made her get right back on the horse, she might not be riding today.

"Get out of my way, Katie," Cindy growled.

Katie was filled with indecision. What did she care whether Cindy ever rode again? If she didn't, then maybe Katie could find a way to get Jester back. But if Cindy didn't get back on the horse again, she might find a way to blame her, and Katie could end up losing her job.

Katie squared her shoulders and crossed her arms, lifting her chin a notch. "No. I'm not letting you out of this arena until you get back on that horse."

"What do you mean? This is my house. You can't stop me from doing what I want!" Cindy yelled as she put her hands on her hips and gave Katie a furious look.

Katie stood her ground. "Yes, I can, and I will." It felt good to stand up to her. "Look, Cindy, I know what it's like to be afraid after having an accident. But if you don't get back on that horse right now and prove to yourself that you can do it, you might not ever ride again."

Cindy drew herself up to her full height. "I'm not afraid to ride. Where did you get such a stupid idea?"

"Then prove it. Put your foot in that stirrup like I

showed you and get back on that horse." She could see Cindy's hands shaking on the reins. It took a lot of courage to get back in the saddle after a fall, but it had to be done. Katie stepped forward, grabbing Jester's bridle. "I'll hold him for you."

Cindy looked at her with determination. "I'm not afraid, you know."

"Yes, I know. I'm just going to steady the horse while you practice mounting. Gather your reins and get your hands into position," she encouraged. "That's it," she said when Cindy was in the proper place. "Now give a little hop."

"Are you sure the saddle is on tight enough?" Cindy said as she stood poised with her foot in the stirrup.

"Yes, it's good and snug. Just think of springing into the air, not pushing downward."

Cindy gave a couple of hops, then vaulted herself up into the saddle. It was a decent attempt for a first try.

Katie smiled at Cindy's accomplishment. "There, do you feel the difference?" she asked, and Cindy nodded. "Now let's dismount and try it again."

"But I just got up here," Cindy whined.

"I know, but I want to be sure you've got it right. When you dismount, I want you to swing your right leg out of the saddle and pause for a moment at the top with both hands resting in the same place as when you mounted. From that position, remove your left foot from the iron before you slide down. You don't want to have your foot in the stirrup when you hit the ground, because your horse could spook and take off, dragging you along with him."

Cindy shivered. "I get the picture." She dismounted the way Katie directed, then tried the remount. It went more smoothly this time.

"See, you learn quickly," Katie said, and Cindy beamed at her. "Now let's try a walk around the arena."

The smile instantly disappeared from Cindy's face. "Why don't we save this for tomorrow? You've taught me a lot already. Let's call it quits on a good note."

"Come on, Cindy. It's just a walk. I know you can do it. Cluck to him and ask him to move."

Cindy started the horse forward, but her fear made her clutch at the reins. Jester tossed his head around, trying to loosen her death grip.

"Ease up on the reins," Katie said.

"But what if he takes off with me?"

Katie spread her arms, indicating the fence. "Where's he going to go? We're in an arena. Just relax and loosen the reins so he'll quit fidgeting."

Cindy did what she was told, and Jester immediately settled into a nice walk. "That's much better," said Katie.

Cindy walked the horse around the arena several times. When Katie could see that Cindy was starting to relax, she asked her to ride in small circles. "Cindy, when you hit the next corner, I want you to circle him to the left. Make a big circle."

As horse and rider approached the spot, Katie could see Cindy tense up. She jerked Jester's head to the left and the horse immediately obeyed, turning a small, tight circle.

"Hold it," Katie said as she walked up to the pair. Cindy was looking displeased again. Katie knew she wouldn't be able to hold Cindy's attention much longer. How was she going to explain this without setting Cindy off?

"Jester has a very tender mouth," Katie explained. "It doesn't take much to cue him. A big action will get a big reaction out of him." She looked up to see if Cindy was paying attention. The look the girl gave her said that her patience was wearing thin.

"I'm ready to go back to the barn," Cindy said sullenly.

Katié wondered if she should just drop the whole thing. Was it worth the effort? Cindy never appreciated anything anyway. Just then, Mr. Ellis stepped up to the fence.

"How are you girls doing?" He looked from one to the other.

"Just fine, Daddy....What were you saying, Katie?" She looked down at her as if there was nothing else in the whole wide world that she would rather be doing.

Katie wondered how the girl could change moods so quickly. She knew Cindy wasn't really interested in what she had to say. But as long as Mr. Ellis was standing there watching, she was going to take advantage of the situation.

"I was saying that you don't need much pressure to make Jester turn." She grabbed the section of rein between Cindy's hands and the bit. "This is all the tension you need," she said as she pulled the reins gently so that Cindy could get the feel. "At the same time I want you to give him a little squeeze behind the girth with your outside leg, and give him some support at the girth with your inside leg. That will move him into the circle." She stepped back. "Now circle him around the arena and try it again."

Cindy gritted her teeth and pasted on a smile for her father. This time when she reached the corner, her cues were much gentler and Jester made a nice circle. "I did it!" Cindy smiled triumphantly. "I want to do another one."

She rode to the next corner of the arena and made another circle. Jester behaved perfectly. When they finished, Katie called it a day.

"You're looking better already," Mr. Ellis said. "Katie, how would you like to continue this for a while? I'll add a little extra to your paycheck."

She groaned inwardly. The last thing in the world she wanted to do was spend more time with Cindy. She didn't dare look back at the girl, but she could feel Cindy's eyes shooting daggers. She opened her mouth to speak. "Well–"

"Good, then it's all settled." Mr. Ellis slapped his hand on the fence post and turned to leave.

Katie looked around at Cindy. Her face was puckered into a frown, but she didn't seem to be too angry. Katie shrugged her shoulders. "Sorry. I guess we'll just have to make the best of it. At least we got you back on a horse today." She turned to leave before Cindy vented any more of her wrath.

"Katie, wait." Cindy dismounted and walked Jester up to stand beside her. She shifted her weight from one foot to the other, looking down at the ground. "Sometimes I can be kind of a jerk." She lifted her eyes to Katie's.

Katie knew this was the only kind of apology she was going to get. Cindy never apologized to anyone. Katie nodded her head. "It's okay." She smiled and opened the gate to leave. "I'll see you Monday after school."

School. Katie's stomach tightened at the thought. By Monday it would be all over school that she liked Jason. What would Cindy think of that? If she was this difficult to work with now, how bad would she be when she found out Katie had a crush on her boyfriend?

Katie finished raking the straw from the shed row, then she headed home. Monday was going to be a long day.

⊰ Chapter Seven ⊱

On Monday morning Katie woke with a stomachache. She dreaded going to class.

She shuffled out of bed and went to feed the horses. King raised his head and nickered when she entered the barn.

"I wish I could stay here with you all day," she told King as she threw some grass hay into the feeder. Grey Dancer munched happily while King nursed. "I might say I'm sick and come home early. Don't be surprised if you see me at lunchtime."

An hour later, Katie entered the school building with her head hanging low, hoping that no one would recognize her and taunt her about Jason. By third period, not even so much as a word had been said about him. Nobody gave her funny looks or sly smiles. She was beginning to think that perhaps he had stayed home sick.

By last period, she had her confidence back and walked purposefully down the hall to her locker.

"Hi, Katie."

~ Chris Platt ~

She whirled at the sound of Jason's voice. Hugging her textbooks tightly to her chest, she hoped they would muffle the sound of her galloping heart. He was standing by his locker with several of his friends. Katie peered into each of their faces, searching for hints that they knew of her affection for Jason. They just smiled back at her in an unassuming sort of way.

"Need any help with that colt today?"

She relaxed a little and found her voice. "No, thanks. We're doing just fine."

"We'd be glad to help too," his friends chimed in, elbowing each other as they passed their comments back and forth.

"Knock it off, guys," Jason warned as some of them began to snicker.

Katie didn't know what to say or do. Boys could be so confusing. Her face felt as if it were on fire. She turned from their smirking faces and quickly opened her locker and grabbed the textbook she needed, tossing the rest of her armload carelessly to the bottom of the locker. She slammed the door shut and ran to her last class, their laughter still ringing in her ears.

When the final bell rang, she quickly gathered her things and hurried to the school bus. She had work to do at the Ellis farm, and today was another lesson day for Cindy. That would be enough to keep her mind occupied.

Jester was tacked and ready to go when Katie arrived. Cindy was sitting on a bench trying to look uninterested, but Katie could see the sparkle in her eyes. She studied the girl cautiously, trying to determine whether the glint was anticipation or anger. If Jason had told Cindy about what he had discovered while eating dinner at Katie's place, Cindy would make her life miserable.

"Hello," Katie ventured uneasily.

"You're late. Let's get this over with," Cindy said, feigning boredom.

Katie was puzzled. Cindy didn't seem to know anything about her crush on Jason. Yet most guys Jason's age would have blabbed to the whole world if they found out a girl had a crush on them. It didn't make sense, but Katie counted her blessings. "What do you want to work on today?"

Cindy shrugged. "Whatever." She untied Jester's reins and headed for the arena. Katie closed the gate after them and watched Cindy mount.

"Your mount looks much better today," Katie said. Cindy seemed to warm a little at the praise. "Let's start him walking to the left. Remember what I said about using your hands and legs. Easy on your cues."

Cindy circled the horse to the left, then to the right. Both horse and rider appeared much calmer than they had during their first lesson.

"Okay, I want you to circle him back to the left. Then, when you're ready, ask him for a trot," Katie instructed.

Cindy turned Jester and waited until she got around the corner of the arena before asking the horse for a trot. The transition was a bit rough, but it was passable. Katie watched from the center of the ring. Jester's first few strides were okay, but then horse and rider seemed to fall apart. Jester took advantage of his loose reins and stretched his neck and stuck his nose in the air, while Cindy flopped around on top of him, posting two strides on the beat, and three strides off rhythm with her mount.

"What are you doing?" Katie yelled.

Cindy gave her a withering stare. "I'm trotting, just like you asked me to."

"Stop him, please." She motioned Cindy to the center of the arena. "Do you feel comfortable at a trot?"

Cindy wrinkled her nose. "It's not my best gait."

"I can see that." Katie immediately regretted her words when the stubborn glint returned to Cindy's eyes.

"Well, Miss Know-it-all, suppose you tell me exactly what I'm doing wrong." Cindy glared at her.

Katie shifted nervously under the intense stare. "Er...well, you need to start by learning to collect your horse and post in time to his gait. Your reins are too loose, and Jester is all strung out. Then, on top of all this, when you're not in time with him..." She didn't know how to explain this without making Cindy seem like the inept rider she was.

Cindy moved the reins to one hand and put the other hand on her hip. "Are you saying that I don't know how to ride?"

Katie fidgeted. How did she answer that one? The truth would probably get her removed from the farm. "No, I'm saying that I know a better way—one that the show judges like a lot."

That got Cindy's attention. She leaned forward over Jester's neck. "Show me."

Katie was only too happy to explain. They spent the

next hour trying to get Cindy to work with the rhythm of the horse, posting out of the saddle when the horse's inside leg hit the ground, and sitting on the next step. When she finally got the hang of it, Katie called it a day.

Little by little, Cindy began to improve, and by the end of spring, Katie declared her ready for her first show.

"There's a small schooling show at the fairgrounds our second week of summer vacation. I think you're ready to enter some of the English Pleasure and Equitation classes."

"Will you go into the classes with me?"

"Cindy, I don't have a horse, remember?"

"I'm sure Daddy will let you ride the old Appaloosa pony horse. Come on, Katie, say you will."

Katie sighed. The pony horse wasn't really a pony. He was the horse they used to lead the racehorses to the track for their workouts or to the post on race days. She was sure the only reason Cindy wanted her there was to humiliate her in front of her friends. There was no way she could hope to place with the old Appy. He was so gentle anyone could ride him, but the horse was Cindy's responsibility, so he rarely got brushed, and he had burrs in his mane and tail. She would be the laughing-stock of the show. It would be Cindy's only hope of beating her.

"You're not chicken, are you?" Cindy challenged.

Katie pursed her lips and stared into Cindy's gloating face. The girl had always thought she was better than her. She thought this was the way she could prove it. "Okay, I'll do it," said Katie.

She saw the satisfied smirk on Cindy's face and wished she hadn't been so anxious to fall into the brat's trap. She knew better than to let somebody bait her into doing something she didn't want to do. Her own pride had gotten her into this mess. With a sinking feeling, she gathered her things to leave. "I'll bring the entry forms tomorrow."

The days began to lengthen. Katie spent more time after school working at the farm and taking care of King. One afternoon while she was walking by the fence, checking for loose boards, Jason called hello as he rode up on his big black-and-white gelding. She turned down her transistor radio as he approached.

"More fence repair?" he asked as he maneuvered his horse close to the dividing line.

Jason was an excellent horseman. She loved to watch him work his mount. The stocky, well-muscled cutting horse was so different from the finer-boned Thoroughbreds. And cutting horses were so quick. Only a very skilled horseperson with a deep seat in the saddle could stay with them. She would be glad to have Jason around to help when the time came to break King.

"No, I'm just checking to make sure the fence is sturdy."

Jason dismounted. "Hey, that's one of my favorite songs. Can I turn it up?"

Katie watched Jason clamber over the fence and reach for the radio. He cranked up the volume, and the country melody drifted across the field.

"Do you know how to do the horseshoe?" He smiled down at her and extended his hand.

Katie looked at it as if it was something poisonous that was about to bite her. She quickly shook her head and backed up a step. "I–I don't dance," she stammered and took another step away from him.

"Come on, Katie, it's real easy. We'll be flying over this field in no time."

Her heart sank. He had that part right, she thought. She'd be tripping over her own two feet, *and his,* and flying to the ground. There was no way she was going to embarrass herself like that in front of Jason.

"No, really, Jason. I'm not good at dancing. I'm very clumsy. I'd step all over you." He reached out and caught her hand, preventing any further retreat.

"I'm a good teacher. I have lots of patience." He grinned and chafed her hand between his two palms. "Your hand feels like it's been dipped in ice water. I didn't think it was that cold out here."

It wasn't. It was just that all her blood had rushed to her head. She was sure her face was ten shades of purple. She wondered if a thirteen-year-old could have a heart attack.

"Here, give me your other hand," he said as he moved her into the sweetheart position at his side.

"Jason, please..." Katie tried to wiggle out of his grasp, but he held her firm, steadying her like the wild colts she had seen him tame.

"Relax, Katie. This is going to be fun. It's okay if you're clumsy. I won't let you fall."

She looked up into his blue eyes and knew that she could trust him. He wouldn't laugh at her. Maybe just this once she would give it a try. She took a deep, calming breath. "Okay, but don't hold me responsible if I step all over your toes. I warned you I wasn't any good at this."

"The important thing is that you're willing to try." He squeezed her hand and showed her the first steps.

Katie had to admit, it was an easy dance compared to some she'd seen, but she still had a difficult time. On the third repetition, she forgot what she was doing and turned the wrong way, placing the heel of her boot squarely in the center of Jason's foot. She heard the "oooff" and saw him try to hide the grimace that crossed his face.

She was horrified. How could she be so inept?

"Are you all right?"

He nodded his head and shifted his weight to his good foot. She could see he was still in pain. "That's it," she declared. "No more dance lessons."

"Come on, Katie. It's not that bad. So you made a mistake. You were doing really well. We were having fun."

"No." She shook her head adamantly. "I've embarrassed myself enough for one day. And don't you dare tell anyone, Jason Roberts." She marched to the radio and turned it off. She should have known better than to try. She was a klutz, and that was that.

"Katie, you did just fine," Jason assured her.

"Don't pity me." She was tired of people patronizing her because she had a bum leg. If he dared look as though he felt sorry for her, she would pick up another pinecone and bean him.

Jason looked her in the eye. "You know I would never do that, Katie."

Katie lowered her gaze to the ground. What a bone-head she was. She knew Jason wasn't like that. Why was she behaving like such an idiot? Because you like him, and you just made a complete and total fool of yourself in front of him, her mind screamed. Why couldn't she ever do anything right when she was around him?

There was an awkward silence, then Jason changed the subject.

"So how're things going at the Ellis farm?"

She was glad he'd steered the conversation to safer ground. "Great. I'm learning a lot. Cindy is doing really well with her lessons. You'd be proud of her."

Jason gave her a funny look that she couldn't fathom. "I'm happy for her. You've got more patience than I do. Cindy can be very hardheaded at times."

"I guess you would know."

Jason gave her that blank stare again. She wondered why he was acting so strangely. Maybe his foot still hurt and he was sorry he had come here today.

"How's the colt coming? Do you need me to come over and help with anything?"

Katie was baffled. Whenever she was around Cindy, the girl talked nonstop about Jason, but he rarely said a word about her. Cindy knew that Jason visited Katie's house occasionally, and it was on those days, when Cindy was in a jealous tantrum, that she was the hardest to get along with.

"Doesn't it bother your girlfriend that you spend time at my house?" She peered curiously up at Jason's face, trying to read what was in his eyes. What she saw was genuine puzzlement.

"Girlfriend? What girlfriend?"

"Cindy."

"Cindy Ellis?"

Katie nodded.

"What makes you think Cindy is my girlfriend? Did she tell you that?"

Katie shrugged nonchalantly. She saw no reason for Cindy to lie to her. "Well, I did see you holding hands that day at her farm."

Jason climbed over the fence and mounted his horse. "The only reason I was over there is because my dad is trying to negotiate a deal with Mr. Ellis so we can breed some of our mares to his stallion. What you saw was Cindy grabbing my hand and dragging me around. She's only a thirteen-year-old girl. Why would I want her for a girlfriend?"

Katie sucked in her breath, feeling as though she had been slapped. Only a thirteen-year-old girl... *She* was only a thirteen-year-old girl. Sure, he was talking about Cindy, but she got the hint—he was telling her not to get her hopes up. Especially now that he knew what a clumsy idiot she was.

He didn't have to put it to her so bluntly. She would have been content just to be his friend. Her face felt hot, and she could feel the tears swimming in her eyes.

"Katie?"

She looked up at Jason but couldn't focus on his face.

Oh, what she would give for a big fat pinecone right now. She had to get out of there. Jason couldn't see her crying. She wouldn't give him the satisfaction. Spinning around, she took off at a dead run toward her house, ignoring the pain that shot up her leg.

"Katie, wait!" Jason yelled after her as he kicked his mount into motion. "Katie, I didn't mean…"

She cut across the pasture fence knowing that he couldn't follow her. She ran until her legs grew heavy and her lungs burned. Then she fell down in the deep grass and cried.

Jason tried to talk with Katie a few times over the next several weeks, but she resisted his efforts, refusing to look at him when they passed in the hall at school and running and hiding like a coward when he rode by the farm. Eventually, he gave up. Katie didn't know whether to be happy or sad about that. To take her mind off the matter, she redoubled her efforts at the Ellis farm, and with King.

It was difficult working with Cindy now that she knew the girl had lied to her, but Katie needed the extra money that giving lessons brought. She bit her tongue when Cindy started talking about Jason and concentrated on getting through their time together without telling her exactly what she thought of her and her lack of riding ability.

Old John stopped by at least once a week to help Katie with the colt and give her some pointers. King was going through some dramatic changes. Katie turned him and his mother out to pasture every day, and he grew in strength and size. True to the trainer's prediction, King's legs began to straighten. It was only a small improvement at first, but the more the colt ran and played, the straighter his legs became.

One day John pronounced King ready for some more serious lessons, and they set about trying to teach him to pony along beside another horse. It was something he would have to learn if he was to race.

Grey Dancer would be the best horse to teach him with, so Katie put a saddle and bridle on the mare and took her out to the arena to longe. It had been a long time since the mare had been worked. She pranced and danced her way around the paddock at the end of the longe line, her tail held high. When she settled down, Katie mounted up and took her for a few turns around the paddock.

Katie knew better than to take her any faster than a walk or trot. If the mare ever got into her stride, she might take the bit in her teeth and run, and Katie might not be able to stop her. Once a racehorse, always a racehorse.

John and Katie worked the mare and colt around the arena for several days until King got the hang of it. Then John suggested she take them into the back pasture, where King could get more exercise. Katie invited Jan over to ride with her on Saturday.

The weekend came, and while Katie tacked up the gray mare and put the halter on King, she finally told Jan of her confrontation with Jason.

"I think you just misunderstood him," Jan said.

Katie pulled the girth snug, then checked the bridle. "There was nothing to misunderstand, Jan. He pretends my bad leg doesn't bother him. Maybe it does...maybe it doesn't. But he thinks I'm a kid, and that's that. I don't want to talk about it anymore."

Jan gave her that you're-being-unreasonable look, but she remained mute on the subject.

Katie led King out of the stall and handed him to her friend. The colt pawed the ground, anxious to be off.

"Stop it," Jan said, giving a yank on the rope.

King reared, standing on his hind legs and thrashing the air with his front hooves. Startled, Jan fell backward.

"Look out!" Katie yelled, grabbing the lead shank and bringing him back under control.

Jan got shakily to her feet. "What was that? He's never done that before."

"It's a nasty habit he started just this week. John said to really get after him when he does it. It's easy to handle him when he's this size, but if he's still doing it when he's bigger, I'm in a lot of trouble." Katie shook the lead. "I tell you, Jan, raising a colt is nothing like I thought it would be. It's a lot of hard work."

Jan gave her a nervous smile, then stepped forward to pet the colt. "It'll pay off someday. He's just got a lot of energy now."

"I hope you're right."

Katie adjusted the stirrups, setting one a notch higher than the other to accommodate her shorter leg. She might be at a slight disadvantage on the ground, but in the saddle, she could go with the best of them. She mounted Grey Dancer and pulled King up close to the

mare, placing him at his dam's shoulder. It was important to keep the horse ponied in this position. If he got
too far ahead or behind the lead horse, the rider would
lose control and an accident could result.

She waited for Jan to get settled on her own horse,
then they pointed the horses toward the back pasture
and took off at a trot. King enjoyed the exercise. He no
longer had an awkward, shuffling gait. Now when he
moved, his strides were long and flowing. He played at
Grey Dancer's side, nipping his mother in the shoulder
and kicking up his heels whenever Katie gave him
enough line to take advantage of the situation.

Katie slowed Grey Dancer to a walk when they
reached the boundary of the far pasture. Her arm was
aching from trying to keep King under control. The colt
didn't like the slower pace. He jumped around on the
end of the rope, wanting to be free to run with the wind.

Katie muscled him into place, pulling the lead line
close, but in the next instant, King reared and the halter
snapped tight across his nose. He rose even higher, and
the girls watched in horrified silence as he lost his balance, tipping over backward into the fence.

There was an equine squeal of fright, then a resound-
ing thud as King connected with the fence post, the hard
wood catching him in the vulnerable spot between his
ears. Then there was silence.

"King!" Katie screamed as she vaulted off Grey
Dancer. She knelt beside the still form. "He's dead." She
looked up at Jan in disbelief.

The gray mare shifted nervously, nickering to her
foal. "Jan, hold that mare!"

Katie leaned over King, searching for a pulse, but she couldn't find it. She felt she was in a bad dream. Time seemed to slow down, and everything became crystal clear. She could hear the twittering of robins and the lowing of cattle. The sun shone around them, but she felt cold all over. What was she going to do? So much depended on this colt.

Katie bowed her head and turned from the colt's still form, the tears flowing freely down her cheeks. She took one step, then was knocked off her feet as King suddenly came to and began to flounder, his feet striking wildly at the ground as he tried to stand. She blinked to clear her vision. He was alive!

The colt got unsteadily to his feet, swaying and whinnying for his mother.

"He must have knocked himself out when he hit his head," Jan said.

King took one step toward his dam, then broke into a coughing fit. Blood flowed out of his nose, and Katie went into a blind panic. "Oh, no, what do we do?" She reached beneath Grey Dancer's saddle and tore loose the saddle blanket. She tried to use it to stem the flow of blood, but it didn't work. "Jan, ride as fast as you can to the house and tell my mom to call the vet!"

Katie had to step out of the way as the mare crowded close, trying to mother her baby. King took several shaking steps forward. Grey Dancer fell in at his side and led him slowly back toward the barn. Each step of the way, Katie expected him to drop, but he continued to walk, following his dam's footsteps.

The vet got there soon after they got back to the

barn. Most of the blood flow had stopped, but there was still a small amount dripping out of King's nostrils.

"Will he live, Doc?" Katie tried to keep her voice from shaking, but it was a useless effort.

"I can't say right now. He's lost an enormous amount of blood." Dr. Marvin prepared several shots. "I'm going to give him something to help stop the bleeding. The best thing we can do right now is get him into a stall and keep him quiet."

Katie unsaddled the gray mare and brushed her off while the veterinarian finished his work. When he was done, they turned the pair loose in the stall. King immediately lay down to rest. The bleeding had stopped and he was exhausted.

"What do I do, Dr. Marvin?" Katie asked as her mother stepped beside her to put a comforting arm around her shoulder. Katie smiled her thanks, then turned her attention back to the vet. "Is there anything I can do to help?"

"All we can do now is wait and watch. You'll have to keep him quiet and watch him closely. I'll stop by later today to give him more medication. If the bleeding starts again, I want you to call. Here's my beeper number." He scribbled on a piece of paper and handed it to her mother.

Mrs. Durham stepped forward. "Doctor, we can't thank you enough for coming so quickly. I can give you part of the money today, but the rest will have to wait until payday. We hadn't planned on this extra expense," she said apologetically.

Dr. Marvin gave her a warm smile and ruffled Katie's hair. "I tell you what. You make sure I get a copy of the win picture for that big Futurity race that this colt is going to win, and we'll call it even."

Katie reached out and shook his hand. "You've got a deal, Doc."

⇥ Chapter Eight ⇤

King slowly recovered. By the time school was out, he was ready to romp and play again. On the first morning of her vacation, Katie saddled Grey Dancer and led King to the back pasture. This time he was more manageable. He still jumped around and kicked up his heels, but he didn't rear or try to jerk away from her.

When they reached the pasture, Katie threw the tack into a storage shed her father had built on the far acreage, and slapped the mare on the rump. She watched as the two horses streaked away. King was only four months old, but he kept up with his mother's even strides.

Katie was so busy watching the wild antics of the horses that she didn't hear the approach of another rider. It wasn't until Grey Dancer's head snapped up and the mare snorted a warning that she realized they were not alone in the tall grass. The mare and colt cocked their tails in the air and pranced over to the fence to greet Jason's horse.

Katie turned to leave. She still couldn't face him.

"Katie, please wait," Jason called as he stepped off his horse and tethered him to a post. "This may be the last chance I have to speak to you for a while."

She turned on shaky legs and walked to where Jason stood. The blood pounded so loudly in her ears that she could barely hear him speak.

"My uncle in Oklahoma had a heart attack, and I'm going to move down there for a while to help out."

Katie reached out to stroke the gelding's nose. Her hand shook so badly that it reminded her of a butterfly in flight. Jason expected her to speak, but she wasn't sure the words would come if she opened her mouth. She knew he was talking about his favorite uncle. Jason must be hurting pretty badly right now.

She was hurting too. But for Jason she would put aside her burden and try to make his a little lighter. He was staring at her, seeming to will her to speak. She'd stick to a safe subject. "I'm sorry to hear that. I hope he'll be okay. How long will you be gone?"

"Probably a year."

Her heart dropped. A whole year! "What about school? You can't just drop out of school."

"I'll enroll down there. Gee, by the time I get back, you'll be in high school."

She smiled bashfully and nodded, stuffing her jittery hands into her jeans. "By the time you get back, King will be old enough to break."

"I'd like to help—if you need me."

She could feel him studying her face.

"Katie, I never meant to hurt your feelings. I'd like to part as friends."

She saw the honesty in his face and felt like a spoiled brat for treating him the way she had. How could she make him see her as mature when she acted like a child?

Katie looked up into his eyes. This would be the last time she would see him for a while. She didn't want to blink and miss a moment of the way he looked. "Sure, Jason. I'd like that."

He extended his hand over the fence and they shook on it.

"You're special, Katie Durham. I'm glad we're friends. You keep that colt growing, and we'll get him to the races when I come back."

Jason put his foot in the stirrup and mounted up. He smiled and waved good-bye, then gave his horse a poke in the sides. He jetted off across the pasture, glancing once over his shoulder before he disappeared over the hill.

"Just like in the movies," she later told Jan as they sat at the kitchen table, sipping milk and eating chocolate chip cookies.

"I told you you were wrong about him, Katie."

Katie rolled her eyes. "You never give up, do you?"

"Boy. No Jason for a whole year," Jan said.

"We wouldn't see him anyway. He's going to high school, remember? We'll be stuck in junior high."

Jan perked up. "But when he comes back, we'll be in high school, too."

"Yeah, but that seems like forever away." Katie sighed and looked out the window.

"I still can't believe Cindy had the nerve to lie to you

about Jason being her boyfriend. Why would she do that? She had to know we'd find out the truth," Jan said as she reached for another cookie.

"I think she had every intention of making him her boyfriend. How many guys do you know who wouldn't jump at the chance to have Cindy for their girlfriend? I think her plan just kind of backfired somehow."

"Yeah, I guess you're right. I'm glad he didn't fall for her."

"Me too," Katie agreed. "Do you know she still acts like they're going out? I want to laugh at her every time she says something about Jason."

"I don't know why you put up with her," Jan said between bites of her cookie.

"I need the money her father pays me. Raising a colt isn't cheap. Every dime my mom makes goes to pay bills. I have to come up with the money for King. It won't be long until it's time to wean him. Then the feed bill will really go sky-high."

"Money or no, she's going to make you look like a fool when you ride into that show ring on the back of the flea-bitten old Appy."

"He's really not so bad." Katie put down her cookie and smiled mischievously. "I've got ten days to work on him."

Jan sat up in her chair. "What is it? You've got that look in your eye. I've got a feeling it has to do with Cindy, and I think I'm going to like it. Count me in."

"I was just thinking. That old Appy is three-quarters Thoroughbred. He looks like a racehorse with spots. They keep him in good shape—it's just that they never care for his coat. I bet if we cleaned him up, he'd look passable."

"What are you getting at, pal?"

"He's got a good mouth and smooth gaits. I bet if I worked with him a little, we could make a decent showing for ourselves."

Jan smiled. "Good enough to beat Cindy on Jester?"

"Maybe. Jester is well-trained, and Cindy is doing much better with her Equitation, but when she gets upset about something, sometimes she slips back into her old habits. Jester is good, but he can't win on his own."

Jan clapped her hands. "I love it! When do we start?"

Katie picked up the dirty dishes and stacked them in the sink. "We'll have to get him over here so I can work on him, but I don't want Cindy to suspect anything. We can't let her know that he's gone from the farm."

"You could tell Mr. Ellis that the gray mare is sore and you need the Appy to pony King. Cindy has dancing lessons tomorrow. You'll have an extra two hours after school to get the horse out of there. You told me they were breaking in a new pony horse, so they don't use the Appy that much. Once he's gone, Cindy will never miss him. She doesn't pay much attention to the racehorses anyway."

"Brilliant!" Katie hugged her friend. "We start tomorrow."

Old John delivered the Appy the next afternoon. Katie's mother saw the trail of dust the horse van kicked up as it came up the drive and called to her. John unloaded the scruffy-looking steed from the van and led him to a stall.

He looked in on Grey Dancer and King, sweeping the hat from his head and dusting it off before he resettled it.

"This mare doesn't seem to be off in her footing. Where'd you say she was sore?" He turned with a puzzled look on his face, waiting for an answer.

"Well, er..." Katie stammered. "She's not exactly sore." Katie lowered her eyes. She didn't want to lie to John, but how did she explain the truth? Revenge and childish pranks didn't go over well with adults.

John noticed her nervousness, and a small grin tugged at the corners of his mouth. "This wouldn't have anything to do with next week's show, would it?"

Katie lifted her chin and looked him in the eye. "Yes, it does. I'm supposed to ride this old horse in competition with Cindy."

"Well, now, is that so?" John tipped his hat to a jaunty angle. "You know, before this horse came to the ranch, he used to belong to a little girl who loved to show. Of course, that was a long time ago, and who's to say he remembers any of it. She sold him when she bought some big, fancy horse, but as I recall, this old boy won a lot of blue ribbons for that little gal." John smiled as he headed back to the truck. "You just be sure you don't wear him out *ponying* that colt," he teased, then climbed into the rig and left.

Katie threw a flake of hay into the manger, then went to grab her brush box. She stared in dismay at the horse's mud-covered, burr-infested coat. "We've got our work cut out for us, ol' boy. You just keep munching on that hay, and I'll have you done in no time." That was laughable. It would take her several hours to get all of the junk out of his mane and tail. She pulled out the currycomb and rubber curry and went to work.

The tiny metal teeth of the round currycomb bit into the dried mud that clung to the horse's coat. When the dirt was loosened, she used the rubber curry in a circular motion all over his body. The old horse heaved a sigh and relaxed, cocking one hind foot into a resting position as he enjoyed the royal treatment.

"They've been treating you horribly since you were turned over to the pleasure horse area of the farm," Katie said. The Appy's ears flicked back to catch the sound of her voice. "Cindy hasn't been doing her job. I'll have to talk to John about getting you back in the racing barn. Your coat used to be such a beautiful shade of gray. With all of this dirt covering you, you can't even tell you've got a white blanket with black spots. You look all one color."

Twenty minutes later, she had worked all the mud clumps out of his coat. He was still covered in a thick layer of brownish dust, and so was she, but at least you could see what color he was meant to be. Now came the hard part—the burrs. She reached for the mane and tail comb and started to work on the forelock, beginning at the ends of the hair and working upward toward the roots.

"Katie?"

She had been concentrating so hard that she hadn't heard Jan approach. She set down her comb to take a short break.

"Boy, you can really see the change already. Do you

need any help? It looks like you still have a long way to go."

"Thanks, buddy. There's no way I'm going to turn down help on this project. This could be an all-day grooming session by myself."

They set to work, Jan starting on the tail and Katie finishing the forelock and working her way down the mane. When she was finished with that, she reluctantly eyed the burr-infested hair at the back of his fetlocks.

"Why don't we just cut it off?" Jan said. "We've got to trim that hair anyway."

"Good idea. I'll go get the clippers. He needs a bridle path cut, and the whiskers on his muzzle have got to be shaved before the show. Might as well get it all done at once. Then we'll just have to touch him up for the show."

"What's this horse's real name?" asked Jan. "All I've ever heard him called was Appy."

"That's all I've ever known him by." Katie shrugged.

"But he's got to have a name. You don't want to have the ring announcer say, 'And in first place, it's Katie Durham riding Appy!' do you?"

Katie snorted. "Like I'm really going to be called for a ribbon."

"Well, you could," Jan insisted.

"And pigs can fly." Katie laughed again. "The main thing I have to worry about is getting him through the class without any major blunders, like running over the judge. I'll call John tonight and see what his registered name is." She saw the satisfied smirk on Jan's face.

"Only because I need a name for him on the entry form."

"I think this horse might surprise you," Jan predicted.

An hour later, when the horse was brushed, clipped, bathed, and drying in the sun, both girls were amazed.

"Wow!" Jan stood staring at the transformed animal. "Who would have thought there was a show horse under all that mud?" She looked pointedly at Katie. "You still don't think you've got a chance at a ribbon?"

Katie picked up the sweat scraper and sponge, and threw them back into the wash bucket. "I've got to admit, I'm impressed. I've never seen him look this good before. Every time I've seen him in the past, he's been lathered up from a hard day of ponying. But you know as well as I do, Jan, he's got to have good gaits and work with his rider; if we can put it all together, we might have a shot."

"I can't wait to see Cindy's face when she gets a look at this horse."

"You'll have to ask your mom to bring the video camera. This could be a Kodak moment."

They laughed all the way back to the house, and made plans to meet the following day for practice.

The Appy's ears pricked forward when he heard Jan ride up the driveway on her chestnut mare. Katie pulled the girth on the Appaloosa's saddle snug, then checked the fitting of the bridle. "Perfect timing," she called as she waved to her friend. She put her foot in the stirrup and mounted up. "Let's see what this ol' boy can do. Oh, excuse me, he has a *real* name now. Let's see what *Sir Galahad* can do."

"Sir Galahad?" Jan laughed. She paused and looked the two of them over, then nodded her head. "Yeah, I like it. He just might be the knight that carries you to a blue ribbon at this show. Let's get to work."

The next several days were spent practicing the walk, trot, and canter, and riding in circles to get Sir Galahad used to responding to Katie's leg pressure. By the middle of the week, he was bending well in both directions, and looking like a true show horse.

"He's not perfect, but he may be good enough to get one of the lower ribbons...maybe a sixth place or honorable mention."

"Won't that just torque little Miss High-and-Mighty?" Jan chuckled. "I can't wait to see her jaw drop when she gets a load of you two."

"I'll have to tell her that I'm picking the horse up the day before so I can practice on him and that I'll meet her at the show. She won't know that I've had him all week. This is going to be fun." Katie almost felt guilty for pulling this trick on the unsuspecting Cindy. Almost—but not quite.

The morning of the show dawned bright and clear. Katie was up at sunrise, grooming Sir Galahad, and braiding his mane and tail. Their first class was an English Pleasure class, followed by an Equitation class, then bareback Equitation. She didn't want to get there too early and spoil the surprise.

Jan and her mother were supposed to pick her up at seven-thirty. With the half-hour drive to the fairgrounds, they would get there about fifteen minutes before time to enter the ring for the first class. Jan was also riding in several classes.

When Katie was finished with Sir Galahad, she ran into the house to change into her show outfit. Normally, she would wait until they got to the arena, but there wouldn't be time today. Once they reached the show grounds, there would be just enough time to saddle up and get to the ring.

A car horn sounded. Katie picked up her riding helmet and ran out the door.

"I'll be there as soon as I get this lunch packed," her mother called after her. "Good luck, honey."

Jan dropped the loading ramp on the horse trailer. "We've got to hurry."

They quickly loaded Sir Galahad, then drove to the show. When they arrived, they had to search for a parking spot. All the good ones had been taken by the early arrivals.

The fairgrounds were alive with activity. Contestants warmed their horses up in designated areas, while others, who were in later classes, groomed their slick mounts. Horses munched lazily from hay nets and called to their stable mates. Riders pinned their identification numbers to their jackets and did last-minute checks on tack. Katie smiled. She loved this time of year. No school to worry about—just horses, horses, horses!

"Mom, could you run and get our numbers while Katie and I saddle up?" Jan asked.

Just as they climbed from the truck, Cindy rode over on Jester.

"Where have you been? You should have gotten here an hour ago," Cindy chastised. "You'd better hurry. The class begins in ten minutes." She quit grouching and a haughty smile lit her face. "I guess it just took a little extra time to make the old Appy presentable. See you in the ring." She stuck her nose in the air and trotted off confidently.

Jan snorted. "She thinks she's already got this one won."

"Jester did look good," Katie pointed out.

"Yeah, but Jester and her three-hundred-dollar riding boots won't do her a bit of good if she can't stay in the saddle or make him pick up the correct lead."

Just then the announcer gave the first call to the gate.

"Grab the saddles. We've got about five minutes before we go in," Katie said as she picked up her saddle pad and placed it on Sir Galahad's back, then settled the saddle into place. She shortened her left stirrup a notch to accommodate her leg. Jan's mother arrived with their numbers and pinned them to the back of their show jackets.

Under ideal conditions, Katie would have liked to have had an extra hour to ride a new mount around the arena. But although it had been many years since the Appy had been in the show ring, he had been to the Salem Fairgrounds many times to pony Willow Run horses in the races. To him this was just another day's work.

She slipped the bit between Sir Galahad's teeth, then

rechecked her tack and mounted up. "Let's go, Jan. They're opening the gate."

Cindy was at the back of the line of horses, craning her neck to look for them. They were almost beside her before recognition dawned in her eyes, and her mouth dropped open, working like a fish out of water.

"He looks real good, doesn't he, Cindy?" Jan laid the compliment on thick. "Who would have guessed there was a genuine show horse under all that mud and burrs? Good luck in your class."

Cindy snapped her mouth shut and gave them a dirty look. She whirled Jester around and trotted into the ring.

"She doesn't look too confident now," Jan smirked.

"I don't know." Katie watched the determined set of Cindy's shoulders. "Maybe we shouldn't have done this. She's really mad."

"Don't worry about her. She wasn't too concerned for you when she asked you to ride a flea-bitten nag into competition. Her only aim was to humiliate you. Now get in there and do your best."

"You're right, Jan." She gathered her reins and entered the ring at a trot, rising and falling in perfect time to the horse's gait.

There was a half a ring distance between her and Cindy. She could see the girl turning her head to watch her and Sir Galahad. She was tempted to stare back, but she knew she would need all of her concentration to make her horse perform to the best of his ability. "Easy, boy," she soothed as the judge asked them to slow to a walk and reverse direction.

The next command was for the canter. Katie asked the old horse for the gait, but he picked up the wrong lead on the first try. She immediately pulled him back to a trot and tried again. This time he picked up the correct lead. She could only hope the judge's eyes hadn't been on her when they made that blunder.

"Nice going," Cindy sneered as she cantered past them on the inside. "I guess that blows your chance for a ribbon."

Katie wanted to scream at her, but she knew that Cindy was just trying to fluster her. Instead, Katie steadied her mount and listened for the judge's directions. Soon it was time to bring the horses to the center of the ring. She lined Sir Galahad up near one of the ends, just two horses down from Jester, and waited for her turn to back her horse for the judge. When all the contestants had been asked to back up, the judge made a few more marks on his sheet, then sent it up to the announcer.

Katie sat listening to the hum of the crowd as they waited for the results. Although they were in a covered arena and it was cooler than it was outside, a trickle of sweat ran down her neck. She chided herself for being nervous. She shouldn't worry about competing with Cindy. She knew she was a much better rider than the girl. Katie's main concern should be that she did her best with the horse she had to work with. But it *did* matter. If only she hadn't blown the lead at the canter.

Cindy looked over at her and smiled. If the girl beat her, Katie would never hear the end of it. Cindy would brag all over town that she had beat her—and with her own horse!

The announcer broke into her thoughts, calling out the sixth-place winner. It wasn't her, and neither was the fifth. Cindy and Jester were called for fourth place. Katie's heart sank as Cindy gave her a cold smile and trotted out to receive her ribbon.

She sighed. The judge must have been looking directly at her when she picked up the wrong lead. She leaned down to pat the Appy. "That's all right, old man. We did the best we could. I think we did a great job. We've got two more classes to catch them."

She listened to see who picked up the other three places. She didn't recognize the girl who took third place, but she almost fell off Sir Galahad when they were called to collect the second-place ribbon.

She hesitated for a moment, thinking she hadn't heard them correctly. When no other horse moved forward, she nudged Sir Galahad and went to collect her award. She couldn't keep the smile from her face as she trotted from the ring.

"Way to go, Katie!" Jan cried as she rode up to join her.

"Congratulations!" Her mother beamed as she slipped the Appaloosa a carrot.

Cindy rode by with a sulky look on her face. Katie wanted to flash her ribbon at her, but that would be too childish. She knew she was probably the last person Cindy wanted to talk to right now, but she steeled her nerve and rode up alongside Jester. "You did really well, Cindy. That's your first ribbon. You should be proud."

Cindy gave her a withering glare. "It still wasn't good enough to beat you."

"You're missing the point. You should be out there to do your very best with your horse, not to beat everyone. It's nice to take first place, but your aim should be to do as well as possible. You did a good job. You should be proud of yourself." She felt a bit guilty giving that lecture when just minutes before she had been trying to beat Cindy. She should practice what she preached.

Cindy pulled off her helmet and looked at her ribbon. "I guess you're right. We did do pretty well." She met Katie's eyes. "But I still want to beat you. We've got two more classes to go." She plunked her hat back on her head and trotted off.

Katie smirked. There was nothing wrong with a little healthy competition. She turned Sir Galahad and walked back to the horse trailer. They had about twenty minutes before their next class.

By the end of the day, Katie had collected another second-place ribbon and one for third. Cindy also earned two more ribbons, but both were behind Katie's. Mr. Ellis came to their truck after the show.

"Congratulations, Katie. I can't believe this is the same horse we pony off of. He looks great." He reached out to stroke the Appy's neck. "I also want to say thank you for the great job you've done with Cindy. She's not too happy about you beating her, but this is the best she's ever done in a show. There will be a bonus in your paycheck this month."

"Thanks, Mr. Ellis. We worked hard, and it paid off. I'll bring Sir Galahad back to the farm tonight." She waved as he strode back to his own truck and trailer.

"I guess that means I've still got a job," she said to Jan.

"Yeah, but I wouldn't want to be in your shoes. Cindy doesn't take losing very gracefully. If you thought she was hard to get along with before, she'll be even worse now. I'd watch my back if I were you."

Katie considered the warning. Cindy acted a lot tougher than she really was, but it wouldn't hurt to be cautious. She'd have to bite her tongue and be extra nice to the girl. She didn't want to be on the bad side of Cindy Ellis.

⇜ *Chapter Nine* ⇝

Cindy didn't offer her Sir Galahad again, so Katie spent the rest of the show season in the stands watching Jan collect all the ribbons. She didn't mind. She had enough to do without having to worry about getting a horse ready for a show.

After winning her first ribbons, Cindy had convinced her father that she didn't need any more lessons, so Katie was relieved of that duty. It was a good thing, because after Cindy found out that Jason was leaving for an entire year, she became very irritable and snapped at anyone who got in her way. After a while, the only time Cindy ever spoke to her was when she asked if Katie had heard anything from Jason.

Jason *had* written her a couple of letters, but Katie didn't tell Cindy. He talked about the excellent Quarter Horses his uncle raised for racing. He spoke of a swimming pool for horses that his uncle had built for conditioning his racing stock and said that a trainer had installed a similar pool not far from her in Salem.

"Can you believe it?" she asked Jan. "A swimming

pool for horses! Whoever thought of such a thing? Jason says his uncle likes it because it helps build up a horse's wind without pounding on their legs. He uses the pool *and* the track to keep his horses in top form. They've won a lot of races."

Jan sat down on Katie's bed and leaned against the headboard. "I know that place he's talking about. My father is friendly with the owner. Do you want to go look at it?"

"Sure. It sounds really cool."

Jan made a call to her dad. An hour later, the girls and Jan's father walked onto Mr. Simon's place and found the barn that housed his horse pool.

"What's that sound?" Katie cocked her head, trying to determine where the great enginelike huffing sounds were coming from.

"That noise is the horse that's swimming in the pool," Jan's father explained.

"That's a horse?" the girls asked in unison. It was a noise unlike any they had ever heard before, except maybe from an old tractor. There was an explosion of sound like a giant machine puffing out a blast of smoke, then silence, then a repeat of the same noise seconds later.

"That's the horse's breathing." Jan's father steered them in the right direction. "When the horse is swimming, only his head and some of his neck is out of the water. He's afraid to get water in his nostrils, so he takes a big gulp of air and holds it, trying to pinch his nostrils closed. What you're hearing is him releasing his breath and sucking in another one."

They rounded the corner, and there lay the circular pool. It was about forty feet across. At one end was a ramp where the horse could wade in, gradually getting to the deep part. Once he settled into the deep water, he would swim in a circle at the end of a rope—just like longeing, only in water instead of on land. Over the pool, a walkway led to a platform. Mr. Simon was standing on this platform at the center of the pool, holding a rope connected to the horse's halter.

The bell on the timer clock sounded, and the chestnut horse that was swimming in the pool pricked his ears and strained toward the ramp. Mr. Simon guided the tired horse out of the pool. The animal stood there on shaking legs, blowing as if he had just run a race.

"Wow!" Katie exclaimed. "How long does it take them to learn how to do that?" she asked Mr. Simon.

Mr. Simon greeted them, then snapped a lead line on the blowing steed and handed it to Katie while he scraped the excess water from the horse's coat. "They already know how to swim. That comes naturally. The hard part is getting them into the pool. At first, they're afraid. Some of them wade down to the drop-off point and then have to be pulled in. Others barely get their feet in the water before taking a big jump and landing in the middle of the pool."

"You're kidding!" She couldn't imagine that.

"Those are the ones you have to watch out for. This pool is about fifteen feet deep. When horses jump in like that, they usually touch bottom and spring back up to the top like a submarine shooting to the surface. They can hurt themselves if they come up too close to the side of the pool, or they can pull their handler into the water with them. That's the most dangerous situation. But after they learn the rules of the game, they get to liking it. Especially in the summer."

"How old does a horse have to be before it can start swimming?" Katie asked.

"Most of the horses I swim are about two, racing age, but we're also swimming a few colts, trying to give them some muscle and endurance. You don't want to subject their legs to too much pounding while they're still growing."

Katie wondered if maybe she should be swimming, too. If it worked for horses, it might build up her strength without the damage that jogging would do.

Jan elbowed her in the ribs. "That would be perfect for King," she whispered. "Go ahead, ask him."

"Do you let other people swim their horses here?" She crossed her fingers, hoping the answer would be yes.

Mr. Simon finished scraping the water off the horse, then patted him and took the lead shank from Katie's hands. "Most of the horses here are mine, but I make an exception for some of my friends."

Katie's hopes dropped. She didn't even know this man.

Jan stepped forward. "Katie's got this colt with excellent bloodlines, but he was born with crooked legs. They're straightening up, but they're not as strong as they should be. Do you think swimming would do him any good?"

Mr. Simon hooked the horse to the hot-walker, rubbing his chin as he watched the colt circle around the machine. "I don't know. I've never had a crooked-legged horse to work on. But I've swum many a bad-legged horse, and it works great on them. That would be an interesting experiment." He turned to look at Katie. "Would you be willing to give it a try?"

Jan winked at her. Katie bit her tongue to keep from laughing. "Yes, I think it might be worth trying. Could you teach me how to swim him? He's only six months old. I haven't weaned him yet. Does he have to be weaned first?"

Mr. Simon stopped the hot-walker and gave the horse a sip of water. "Yes. It would be too traumatic for him and his dam. We could have some real accidents. You give me a call when you get that colt weaned, and we'll set something up."

"That would be great, Mr. Simon. Thank you."

In the car on the way home, Katie had mixed feelings. She was excited about the prospect of finding something that would help King's legs, but she was also a little apprehensive about weaning the colt. She knew it had to be done. Six months was the perfect age. He was eating hay and grain now, and was growing like the pine trees that dotted the Oregon landscape. The longer she waited, the harder it would be. Now was the time.

She turned to Jan. "Can you help me today?"

"Sure. What do you need?"

"I'm going to wean King."

"Oh, this should be loads of fun." Jan rolled her eyes.

"I'll call John when we get home to see if he can come pick up Grey Dancer. I'm going to miss that mare." She felt the tears pricking her eyes, so she turned to look at the scenery. The hot August sun beat through the car's open window, and a warm wind blew in her hair. It wouldn't be long before school started again. She needed to get King weaned and settled into a new routine before classes resumed.

John arrived early that afternoon. He had several pairs of leg wraps with him. He tossed some of them to Katie and Jan. "Put these on the colt. I'll wrap the mare's legs."

Katie and Jan took the wraps from him. "But the colt's not going anywhere. How come we're putting wraps on him?" asked Katie.

John looked up from his place in the straw at Grey Dancer's feet and paused in his work. "You've been around the farm at weaning time. You know how crazy the mares and colts get. This here colt's pretty strong-willed. He might just take it in his head to go over or through the fence to join his mama. The leg wraps are just an extra precaution. He's got enough trouble with them legs without banging them up any more."

"Should I keep him here in the stall or put him out in the pasture?"

"I think it would be best if we kept him in his stall for now. You can turn him out in a couple of days if he settles down. Get a rope on him and hold him tight till I get this mare in the trailer. If he gets too hard to handle, just take the rope off and get out of the stall. I don't want you getting hurt."

"Maybe we should wait another month or two," Katie said. She hadn't expected weaning to be such a problem.

John led the mare out of the stall and shut the door behind him. "The longer you wait, the worse it gets."

"Maybe we could just let the mare wean him herself?"

"That doesn't always work unless the mare has a new foal at her side. No, now is the best time to do this. King's standing quiet now, but watch out when his dam is out of sight. I'll load her, then come back to see how you're doing."

John and Grey Dancer walked though the barn door. The mare paused and turned her head, whinnying for her foal to follow. Until then, King had been standing fairly quietly. When he heard his mother's call, he pulled against Katie, trying to join his dam.

"Easy, fella," Katie crooned. "Jan, are you sure that door is latched?"

Jan rechecked the lock. "It's secure, but I'm wondering if maybe I shouldn't open it in case you have to come flying out of there. King doesn't look too happy about this."

The bay colt stomped his feet and trumpeted his call to the mare, now in the trailer. John's face appeared above the boards of King's stall.

"How's he doing?"

"Not so good. He wants to go with his mother." From outside, Katie could hear Grey Dancer whinnying and pawing in the trailer.

"Take off that rope and get out of the stall," John

instructed. "I want you to watch him for a little while after I leave. He'll be riled up for the rest of the day, and he'll probably make a lot of noise tonight, but he should settle down in a day or two. If you have any trouble, just give me a call." John turned and left the barn.

Katie patted King on the neck and unsnapped the lead shank, then let herself out of the stall. "You take it easy. Don't go trying to hurt yourself," she said. The truck engine started, and soon she could hear the mare's cries getting fainter in the distance.

When all was silent, King paused in his stall, every muscle taut and quivering. His little fox ears flicked back and forth, trying to capture the sound of his mother. He snorted and called urgently to her, but there was no response.

"Do you think he's going to be all right?" Jan asked.

Before Katie could answer, King reared back on his haunches, coiled like a spring, then shot forward, trying to get over the stall door. His front legs hooked over the door and he struggled to free himself, flinging his head back and forth, bumping it on the doorway.

"Whoa, whoa!" Katie yelled as she rushed forward, waving her arms in an attempt to shoo the colt backward. But he was stuck. His legs continued to beat a tattoo against the wood of the door as he screamed in fright. If she didn't do something quickly, King would break a leg or beat himself to death on the doorframe.

Heedless of the danger of the flailing hooves, Katie reached for one of King's legs, but he tore it from her grasp. A burning sensation crossed her palms as his sharp hoof ripped some of the flesh from her hands.

Katie tried again, grabbing for both legs this time. She pushed them up and over the top of the door when he renewed his struggles.

King fell over backward into the stall. He immediately got to his feet, determined to charge the door again.

"Oh, no, you don't!" Jan pushed Katie to the side, and slammed the top door of the stall shut, throwing the latch into the catch. King thudded against the wood and scurried around the stall. "Are you okay?" she asked Katie.

"Yeah, I think so." Katie examined her torn hands. "It's just some deep scrapes, nothing that needs stitching." She listened to King's cries as he rampaged around the stall. "I never would have thought he would be this wild," she said in disbelief.

"They get pretty crazy when you wean them. He's taking it pretty hard. I think you better leave him locked in tonight."

"What if he hurts himself?"

"He'll be okay. There's nothing in the stall he can cut himself on."

Katie nodded. "I guess you're right. It's a good thing we wrapped his legs, or he wouldn't have any left." She looked back at her own hands. "I think he's come out of this better than I have."

"That looks like it hurts," Jan sympathized. "Let's go into the house and get you cleaned up."

⊰ *Chapter Ten* ⊱

By the end of the week, King was calm enough to work with. Katie's hands still hurt, but they were healed enough to use. She called Mr. Simon and made an appointment to bring over King.

The Simon ranch wasn't far. Rather than bother John about trailering the colt, she borrowed Jan's mare and ponied him to the ranch.

Going down the road was a new experience for King. Fortunately, there weren't many cars, but the first few that passed sent him charging against the rope. When he saw that the fast-moving vehicles didn't bother the older mare, he settled down but pricked his ears in interest each time a car went by.

Katie leaned over and patted King's sleek neck. "You're in for a real treat today." She wiped the sweat from her brow. "I wish I were going swimming with you." It was definitely bathing suit weather. As they walked down the side of the road, Katie wondered if King's legs bothered him. He didn't seem to be limping, but he was a tough little guy. Maybe he had a high tolerance for pain.

"How about it, King, do your legs bother you?" she asked as she reached over to fiddle with his forelock. "Sometimes it's a real pain having to deal with a handicap, isn't it? I know there are days when I don't wear my elevated shoe, and I overdo it. Then the next day, my back hurts so bad, I don't feel like getting out of bed.

"But your legs are getting better, so I hope you outgrow this. And if you don't, then that's okay, too. We're in this together, pal. We're tough. We'll show them what we're made of."

Katie wished it were that simple. King had it better in one respect—he didn't have a bunch of nasty kids to tease him. Kids could be so mean sometimes.

It hurt to be different.

A shout broke Katie out of her thoughts. She looked up to see Mr. Simon waving to them from the barn. "Come on up. We're ready for you."

When Katie and the horses stopped in front of the stable, Mr. Simon let out a low whistle and ran a practiced eye over Willow King.

"This is some piece of horseflesh. Who's his sire and dam?"

Katie shifted in the saddle. She didn't want to lie to the man, but Mr. Ellis didn't want her disclosing King's bloodlines. She cleared her throat. "The breeder made me promise not to tell anyone King's pedigree."

Mr. Simon scratched his head. "That's mighty strange. You'd think with a big, good-looking colt like this, the breeder would be shouting it from the rooftops."

Katie proudly stroked King's neck. "He was born with a problem. The stallion's owner didn't want anyone to know about it." She understood why a breeder would want to keep the colt from the public, but it still galled her how people wanted to shut away or ignore anything that wasn't perfect. Perfection wasn't everything.

"Yes, I remember you saying something about him having crooked legs. They seem to be straightening. In another six months or so, you won't be able to tell." He ran his hand down King's legs, then stood. "Let's get inside, out of this heat."

Katie handed the colt to Mr. Simon, then dismounted and led Jan's mare to a stall. She removed the tack while the mare sank her muzzle into a bucket of water.

"I'm going to take him to the wash rack. I'll meet you there," the stable owner said.

When Katie arrived, King was being given a bath with the hose. She took the lead shank from Mr. Simon. "Why are you giving him a bath if he's going into the water?"

"I want him as clean as possible when he goes into the pool. Extra dirt is hard on the filters. We'll want to pick out his hooves, too."

When King was done with his bath, they took him to the pool. Mr. Simon enlisted the help of one of the stable boys.

"When we get him in and out of here a few times, and he's swimming good, I'll teach you how to do this. The first couple of swims I like to handle with just me and one of my stable hands. A lot of horses get scared and do funny things on their first try."

He picked up a whip and handed it to Katie. "If we can't coax him in, I want you to make a little noise with this thing. You may have to tap him lightly with it."

Mr. Simon snapped a long rope to the left ring of King's halter and ran a rope through the ring on the right side, then positioned him on the ramp. King waded in up to his knees, then stopped and pawed at the water.

"It's okay. Let him get used to it before we ask him to go any farther," Mr. Simon told the stable boy.

King lowered his nose to the water and snorted.

"Come on, boy," the stable owner encouraged, but King balked and tried to back up. "Get after him, Katie. Pop him with that whip."

Katie snapped the whip in the air behind King, and it made a cracking sound. King hesitated for a moment, then fought against the ropes. She tapped him on the rump with the whip and used her voice to try shooing him into the water.

"Make a little more noise back there, Katie. Tap him again. I think he's ready to go."

Katie snapped the whip over King's hips and yelled, "Yah, yah!" King paused for a moment, then gathered his weight on his haunches and sprang forward. He landed ten feet out in the deep water, sinking to the bottom of the pool, almost pulling his handlers in after him.

Katie sucked in her breath and her hands flew to her heart, but in the next instant, King shot to the surface, thrashing about and pawing the water in an attempt to swim.

"Pull him around, Davie," Mr. Simon yelled to his helper.

Davie ran ahead of King on the outside of the pool, pulling the colt around to the exit. Mr. Simon stood on the platform at the center and kept him steadied. Then together they pulled King up the ramp. The colt walked shakily up the incline. He was blowing hard. His nostrils flared as he sucked in great lungfulls of air.

"Boy!" Katie said. "That was really something. Is he okay?"

Mr. Simon leaned over to pat the colt on the neck. "He's fine, just a little shook up. We'll give him a second to catch his breath, then we'll try him again. When he goes in quietly and swims strongly, we'll pull the outside rope through the halter and swim him with just the inside rope. It's just like longeing a horse, except that he's in water."

They did two more test runs with King going in and out of the pool before they let him swim on his own around the pool once. When he reached the ramp, he pulled against the rope, trying to get out. Mr. Simon held him steady, forcing him around again. After three times, they allowed King to exit.

King stepped from the water on shaking legs. His nostrils flared and every muscle in his body quivered.

"He looks exhausted," Katie said.

"He is." Mr. Simon picked up the sweat scraper and scraped the excess water from King's coat. "Swimming is difficult exercise for a horse."

King staggered forward a couple of steps, his legs threatening to collapse.

"I think you'd better hand-walk him till he's cooled out. I'll fix you a stall so he can stay here tonight. It doesn't look like he'd make the walk home."

Katie appreciated Mr. Simon's kind offer. "Thank you. I think you're right about that. Will he always be this tired?"

"No. It's usually just the first couple of swims. They get nervous, and it takes more energy out of them than they would normally use. A couple of days from now, this colt will be swimming like a champion. He'll put on a lot of muscle. We can build his endurance up without putting unnecessary pressure on those legs."

Katie walked King until he was dry, then put him into the stall that had been prepared for him. When she rode off on Jan's mare, he nickered at their departing forms, but he was too tired to put up much of a fuss.

The next day, Mr. Simon taught Katie how to swim a horse. He started her with one of the older horses that loved the water. She stepped onto the walkway that led to the center platform and coaxed the horse down the ramp. The big gelding walked into the water and pushed off into the pool, his powerful legs churning the water.

At Mr. Simon's instruction, she picked up the longeing whip that was used to discourage the horse from coming in too close to the platform.

"We've hung pieces of carpeting down from the platform to make the horses think it's solid, but if one of them ever gets up under there, he could wrap himself around that pole and drown, or at the very least, crack his legs against the hard metal and hurt himself," the stable owner said.

Katie noticed that when the horse grew tired, he

tended to angle in toward her. Several times she had to slap the whip against the water to keep the horse in the center of the pool. When the gelding was finished, Mr. Simon brought King out.

"I'll get him started, but I want you to come out on the platform so you can take over for me," he said.

Katie helped get King into the water, then ran to take over at the center of the pool. The colt could only endure one minute in the pool, but he behaved perfectly for Katie.

By the end of the week, King was up to three minutes, and Katie finally had the hang of getting him in and out of the pool. King even had enough energy to pony home and kick up his heels along the way.

Once school started again, Katie had so much homework that she had to cut their trips to the pool down to once or twice a week. When the weather turned cold, they would have to stop altogether. But by then King's legs would be strong and straight enough to endure more ground training.

In October, she ponied King to the Simon ranch for the last swim of the season. The rain-swollen clouds hung low in the sky and threatened to burst. Katie hoped they would hold off until she was safely home and King was tucked into his cozy stall.

As she snapped the swimming rope onto King's halter, her thoughts wandered over the school day and all the homework that awaited her when she returned home. She wondered how Jason was doing in his new school. She led King into the water and walked out onto the platform. The colt was up to ten minutes now, and was a joy to swim.

While she waited for the timer to announce the end of the workout, Katie mentally ran over the notes for her upcoming history exam, but thoughts of Jason kept edging out facts about the Lewis and Clark expedition. She remembered the day in the field when he had tried to teach her to line-dance. How could she have been so clumsy? She had actually stepped on his foot!

The memory embarrassed her all over again. She should have known better than to try. She couldn't dance. She was an accident waiting to happen on the dance floor, but she had let Jason talk her into it. Never again. One good dose of humiliation was enough. At least it hadn't taken place at a school dance, where there would have been a hundred witnesses.

The rope in her hand grew slack, alerting her to the fact that King was growing tired and starting to drift inward. "Get up there, boy. You can do it. Just three more minutes to go."

At the sound of her encouraging voice, King picked up the pace and swam back to the center of the pool. Katie studied the colt, and an uncomfortable thought crept into her mind. She and King had a lot in common. They both had obstacles to overcome. Every time King made progress, she was thrilled for him. They made a great team. But there was one area where King excelled: King was no quitter. No matter what it was he faced, he never gave up. She could learn a good lesson from this colt.

Her mind returned to Jason. She remembered how

much fun dancing had been at the start—before she had trampled on his foot—when they had stood side by side in the sweetheart position and laughed as he ran her through the steps. She mentally ran through the steps again, then performed them on the platform grate to the rhythmic blowing of King's breathing as he chugged around the pool. She could do it. Maybe if she practiced really hard, she could have it down perfectly, so when Jason finally came home...

Katie didn't notice that King was swimming toward her until she heard the muffled scrape of his halter on the rugs that encircled the platform. Her heart lurched as she picked up the whip and poked him with it, trying to get him away from the platform. She quickly pulled in the excess line to keep it from becoming wrapped around his legs, but it snagged on the back of the carpet barrier.

Unable to return to the center of the pool, King swam back toward the platform.

Panic took hold of Katie as she dropped to her knees, trying to untangle the rope from the carpeting. The metal grate bit into her knees and palms. She leaned forward, tugging at the rope. King's heavy breathing echoed in her head as he thrashed around the platform, looking for her to help him. Her heart beat so hard, it seemed ready to leap through her chest.

She splashed water at King to keep him from coming any closer. "Help!" she yelled, but no one was within hearing distance. There wasn't time to run and get someone. King was tiring fast. The timer had already gone off, and he was past his normal amount of exercise. If she didn't do something soon, he would wrap himself around the pole and drown.

Saying her prayers, Katie balled the rest of the rope into one hand and leaned way over the side, pulling the excess length of the line free of each of the hanging pieces of carpet. She worked quickly, trying to ignore the pain in her knees and the sick feeling in the pit of her stomach. When she had untangled the last length of rope, she jerked it from between two of the rugs and shooed King out to the middle of the pool. He finished the round and walked up the ramp, staggering out of the pool.

King shook the water from his coat, then stood with his chest heaving. Katie burst into tears, ran off the platform, and threw her arms around his neck. "I almost got you killed!" she sobbed. King nickered and poked her with his nose as if to assure her that he was fine. She stroked his wet head. "I'm so sorry, boy. My daydreaming got you into trouble. I'm glad this was your last swim, because I don't know if I would trust myself again."

It seemed it didn't matter if Jason was here or not. Just thinking of him made her do stupid things.

With shaking hands, she scraped the water from King's coat and put him on the hot-walker to cool out.

Mr. Simon walked into the barn and took in her soggy appearance. "What happened to you? It looks like you went for a swim with him."

"Uhh, n-nothing," she stammered. She didn't want Mr. Simon to know what a fool she had been. She had learned her lesson; a horse required one hundred percent of a person's attention, and anything less could result in disaster. She'd never let it happen again. "I just want to say thanks for letting us use your pool. This will be our last time. King looks great, and he's really developing. The swimming has done him a lot of good."

She almost choked on her last few words. The pool work had done him good, but her lack of attention had almost cost King his life. She snapped the lead line on King and led him out of the barn. "It's been quite a day, boy. Let's go home."

Winter came with its pouring rains, and Katie was forced to stay inside most of the time. On the few dry days they had, she worked with King, reinforcing the lessons he had learned. He grew tall and straight. There was little evidence of his formerly crooked legs.

In late spring, when the grass grew thick and wildflowers covered the pastures, Mr. Ellis phoned to say he had King's registration papers and that he would drop them by her house. He hadn't seen the colt since King had left the farm shortly after his birth.

Old John had advised Katie to say nothing specific about the colt until after she had the papers safely in her hands. She never asked why but suspected that Mr. Ellis might want to change his mind after he saw the awesome horse King had become.

No longer was he the weakling colt with the crooked legs. He was just over a year old, and already he stood just shy of fifteen hands high. With one hand being equal to four inches, King was five feet tall at the withers—taller than the top of Katie's head.

His legs were straight and sturdy, and the time spent walking, swimming, and exercising had developed his muscles. He had taken on the true bay coloring of his father, and his coat was sleek with good health. John assured her that King was far superior to the colts at Willow Run Farm.

Mr. Ellis arrived just after lunch.

"Here're the papers, Katie." He put the blue-edged, folded paper from the jockey club into her hands.

Katie traced the lettering with her fingers. *Willow King out of Grey Dancer by Beau Jest.* He was now officially hers.

"I'd like to see this colt if I could. John says his legs have straightened some."

Some? Mr. Ellis was in for a big surprise, she thought as she tucked the papers into a drawer, then led the way to the barn.

"If you want to wait by the front paddock, I'll bring him out for you."

She led King from the barn and turned him loose in the pen. The colt bowed his neck and held his tail high, prancing around the field as if to mock his breeder.

Mr. Ellis tipped his hat back and let out a low whistle. "This is the colt I gave up?"

"The one and only," Katie said, feeling safe now that she had his papers.

"Can you get a lead rope on him so I can have a look at those legs?"

"Sure." Katie caught King and brought him to stand in front of Mr. Ellis.

The stable owner ran his hands down the colt's legs,

checking the bone formation and testing the tightness of the tendons. "If he didn't resemble his sire so much, I'd say you'd run a ringer in on me. It's hard to believe this is the same colt that could barely stand and nurse. Turn him loose and let me see him move again."

Katie unsnapped the rope and shooed King away. He obliged by taking a running start and speeding his way around the paddock.

"Look at him go," Mr. Ellis said with a smile, then his tone grew serious. "Would you be interested in trading him back for Jester? I know you miss him, and Cindy hasn't had much luck with him since that first show."

Katie tried to keep the irritation out of her voice. Mr. Ellis hadn't wanted the colt when he was born, but now that he'd grown into the horse his bloodlines had foretold, he wanted him back.

"I would love to get Jester back, but I'll have to wait until your lease on him expires. This colt and I have come too far to give him up now."

"So you do intend to race him?" Mr. Ellis sounded relieved.

"Oh, yes. You're looking at the future winner of the Portland Downs Futurity!" Katie smiled proudly and called King over to the fence.

"I'm glad to hear you say that. He's too much animal to make into a saddle horse. This colt belongs on the track." He turned from watching Willow King, and his tone was all business. "Katie, when the time comes to start training this horse, I'd love to have him in my stable."

He must have seen the apprehensive look in her eyes because he rushed to reassure her.

"No, Katie, this colt is yours. You had faith in him when no one else did, and you've turned him into a fine piece of horseflesh. But you're going to need someone to help with getting him to the track. We've got everything you need at Willow Run. I'm sure John would love to take you under his wing and teach you how to train a racehorse. You're there almost every day anyway. We'd be proud to have you two as part of our racing stable."

"Thank you, Mr. Ellis," Katie said with a smile. "We'd love to."

School was out once more, and another summer stretched lazily before her. This fall she would be a sophomore in high school–and Jason would be a junior. He had written her more letters. She kept them secreted away in the back of her closet. His last letter said that he would return sometime at the end of summer vacation.

Katie filled her summer with picnics, working at the stable, and days at the lake with her mother and Jan. She spent as much time with King as she could. He was a year and a half old now. As the summer wore on, she started taking him to the back pasture to work with him. She knew that when Jason finally came home, this is where he would look for her. Besides, she liked to work with King away from the prying eyes of the trackmen from other Thoroughbred farms. She noticed how they drove by her house slowly when King was in the front paddock. Occasionally, one of them would stop and question her about the colt.

Now that King's legs were straight, Mr. Ellis didn't mind people knowing that the horse was from Willow

Run Farm, but he thought it best that people not know too much about the colt.

"The less people know about him, the more surprised faces there are going to be when he walks away with his first race," he said.

It wouldn't be long now before King would be taught to carry a rider. John liked to break the colts in the late fall before their second year. Nothing strenuous, since their bodies weren't fully developed and the cartilage in their knees wasn't yet closed. But they were broke to the saddle, and they learned the basics of steering and stopping. After a month of easy lessons, they were turned out to grow until late spring, when they would begin serious training for the races.

Old John didn't like running his two-year-olds early. Some trainers started racing them in the spring, but John managed to stall Mr. Ellis until fall, convincing him that it was in the horse's best interest to do so. Running a colt too early caused leg injuries that would stay with him all of his life, and often shortened his racing career. If John had his own way, the old trainer would prefer to wait until they were three-year-olds before racing them.

To make the process easier, Katie began getting King used to the saddle and bridle. John loaned her an old exercise saddle and a bridle with a rubber snaffle bit, which would be easier on a young horse's mouth than plain steel. Each day she put the equipment on King and led him around the pasture.

Since she couldn't ride him yet, Katie had to teach King to respond to the bit from the ground. She tried hooking long ropes to the bit so she could drive him from behind like a plow horse. She had seen the other horsemen in her neighborhood do it. They made it look so easy, but every time she attempted it, King tried to turn around so he could see her, and he became hopelessly tangled in the ropes.

It was easier for both of them if Katie stood at his shoulder with one arm reaching over his neck to hold the rein on the side. In this manner she could make him go right, left, and stop. He was a quick learner, and he wanted to please.

One day in the late summer, Katie was longeing King in the back pasture when suddenly the colt came to an abrupt halt, his nostrils flaring as he snorted a warning. Katie knew there was only one person it could be. She turned her head and saw a streak of black and white racing toward them. She lifted her hand to her eyes, blocking out the sun's blinding rays. Her heart pounded as she caught the red-gold glint of Jason's head. He was home!

What was she going to say to him? It had been over a year since she had seen him face-to-face. Jason brought his horse to a sliding stop, then leaned on the saddle horn and pushed the brim of his new cowboy hat up over his eyes. He winked at her, and she smiled. She had been worried that he might have changed, but except for the new hat, he seemed like the same ol' Jason.

"Howdy, ma'am," he said in a deep voice as he swiped the hat from his head.

Katie stared at him. She knew her mouth was hanging open, but she couldn't seem to shut it. He sounded just like John Wayne in one of those old westerns that her mother liked to watch. He couldn't possibly have changed *that* much, could he?

Suddenly, Jason burst out laughing and stepped down from his horse. "Had you fooled, didn't I? You're still so gullible, Katie," he said, tying his horse to the post.

"And you're still an infuriating monster." Katie picked up a pinecone and threw it, purposely missing him by a mile.

"Looks like both of you have grown up." Jason climbed over the fence and came to stand beside her.

She could feel her cheeks burning pink, so she quickly turned her attention to King. "Isn't he a beauty?"

He looked at her for a second longer, then turned to the colt. "He's a nice piece of hide." Jason ran his hands over King's well-muscled shoulder. "Has Ellis seen him yet?"

"Yeah. He was here a couple of months ago. He wanted to know if I would trade King back for Jester."

"Are you kidding? You did say no, didn't you? I mean, I know that Jester means a lot to you, but you've had faith in this colt when no one else did, and you've worked so hard." At her nod he stood back to take a better look at the colt. "You know, I used to have my doubts when you'd tell me that this was the future winner of the big race, but now I think you just might have a shot at it. Do you still want some help breaking him?"

Katie reached up to uncinch the saddle and remove the bit from King's mouth. She slapped him on the rump and watched as he rushed off, bucking and kicking as he went. "You think you can stay with that?"

Jason put his new hat back on his head and plucked a blade of grass to put between his teeth. "I learned a lot from those Oklahoma cowboys this past year. I think I can manage it."

Katie stepped up and extended her hand. "Welcome to Willow King's training team. John and I are happy to have you aboard."

⇥ *Chapter Eleven* ⇤

"Hold him, Katie," Jason warned as King tried to jump out from under him. It was a crisp November morning, and his breath came out in wispy clouds when he spoke.

Katie steadied the older pony horse, then took a firm grip on King's lead shank.

"Don't let him buck," Jason warned as he dismounted from King. "We don't want him learning how to do that."

So far, King had been pretty easy to break. Jason was able to ride him at a walk, then a trot, and he always wanted a pony horse along for company. The older horse had a calming effect on the younger one. They needed all the help they could get. King was now approaching sixteen hands high. He was large for his age, and he was becoming quite a handful, but Jason was a skilled horseman.

Now that they had come to the end of his thirty-day breaking period, Katie would finally get her chance to ride King. She had been bugging Jason all month, insisting that since she had gone through all the trouble of *raising* the colt, she should at least get a chance to *ride* him!

On the other hand, with the way King was acting this morning, she wasn't sure it was such a good idea.

Katie was nervous when she dismounted from the pony horse, put her foot in King's stirrup, and climbed into the saddle. King must have sensed her emotions, because he shifted uneasily under her weight. "I don't know, Jason. Are you sure I'm up to this? What if I make a mistake?"

"Relax," Jason said as he adjusted the stirrup irons for her. "You're just going to take him for a walk around the ring. If he feels like he wants to take off or buck, pull his head into the fence and stop him."

Katie forced a brave face. She had been waiting for this day forever. She needed to remind herself that she was a good horsewoman. The only difference between riding him and Jester was that King was more unpredictable and had to be closely watched. Jester had bucked with her before and she hadn't been unseated.

She remembered a piece of advice one of the exercise riders at Willow Run had given her: *Never fall asleep on a young horse. Stay alert and stay in control.* She smiled at Jason and picked up the reins.

King walked around the arena with her. He tossed his head when she held too tightly on to the reins, then tried to break into a trot when she gave him too much of his head. She finally found a happy medium, and King moved expertly under her touch.

"I want to trot him," Katie said.

"Gather your reins tighter, then cluck to him," Jason

instructed. "Racehorses are taught to pull against the bit. Give his head a little bit of support."

Katie choked up on the reins, just enough to put a nice bow in King's neck, and gently pressed his sides. The colt broke into a smooth trot. She marveled at the power she felt in his strides. He was going to be a champion, she just knew it. "Can I canter him?" she called out to Jason.

"I don't know, Katie," Jason replied. "I haven't done a lot of work with him on that yet. He still hasn't really learned to balance a rider at a lope. He's pretty clumsy."

"What do you mean, 'clumsy'?" she said, keeping her eyes on the space between King's ears. "He's floating like a butterfly." She ignored Jason's warning and asked King for a canter. He responded by making a sudden lurch forward, which set her farther back in the saddle. King mistook the resettling of weight as a cue to slow down, and he abruptly tried to stop.

Katie knew she was in trouble but was helpless to do anything about it. She saw the trees pass in a blur of green as she was vaulted over King's shoulder, then she hit the ground with a bone-jarring thud. When her vision cleared, she could see King standing in front of her with a look that said, *What are you doing on the ground when you're supposed to be on my back?*

Jason rushed to her side. "Are you all right?" he asked as he helped her to her feet and dusted her off.

"My pride's a little bent, but I think all my bones are intact."

"Looks like the Stooges are back in action again."

Katie gave him an angry look as she reached out to grab King's dangling reins.

"Come on, let me help you back up." Jason readied the stirrup for her.

"What do you mean, get back up? I'm a little sore and I'd like to go home and take a hot bath." The truth was, her hip was throbbing so badly that it was taking all her will power not to grimace. But she didn't want to admit that to Jason. She hated it when people acted like her handicap made her helpless. She couldn't stand it if she saw that look in Jason's eyes.

"Oh, no, you don't. You're going to climb right back on this horse and make him do what you wanted him to do. Then, once you *both* get it right, you can take your bath. Even though King didn't intend to dump you, if he gets away with it, he might learn that unseating his rider is a good way to get back to the barn quicker. You get on this horse and lope him around the ring a couple of times."

"But he's not very good at it—you said so yourself," Katie protested. She had never been afraid to ride before, but the spill had made her wary. "What if he does it again?"

Jason put a hand on her shoulder, trying to calm her. "Katie, this is for both you and the horse. If you don't get back on him now, you may never do it, and I know how important it is that you have an active part in King's training. Just listen to what I tell you and you'll be fine. Okay?"

She remembered when she had given Cindy this

speech after she had fallen off Jester. If Cindy could do it, so could she. "Okay," she said, ignoring her pain and gripping the reins with trembling fingers. She mounted.

"Now pick up his head and walk him in a small circle until you feel you're in control. That's it," he encouraged her. "When you feel comfortable with that, make the circle bigger and ask him for a trot."

Katie did as she was told. She could feel King relaxing under her. The colt hadn't dumped her out of meanness—she had given him confusing cues. She felt more confident in her abilities and picked up the pace a little.

"Whenever you're ready, collect him so he isn't so strung out, then ask him for a canter."

She did as Jason suggested and smiled triumphantly when King broke into an awkward but rhythmic lope. She rode him in a few circles, then eased him back to a walk, coming to a halt before Jason. "That was fantastic!" she said as she slipped from the colt's back and patted him on the neck. "What a rush!"

"Well, I don't think you two are ready for the Kentucky Derby, but I guess it's a start," Jason said. "Let's call it a day. Another couple of training sessions and we can turn him out for the winter. Next spring is when the real training starts."

Homework and high school activities kept Katie busy for the remainder of the winter. Willow King was scheduled to be delivered to Willow Run Farm in early May to begin his training for the fall races.

In late March when the weather warmed, Jason suggested they start doing some trail riding with King to get him legged up and give him a little experience before he went to the racetrack.

Jason rode King several times in the ring to reinforce the lessons he had been taught in the fall. Then the horse was turned over to Katie.

"You want me to ride him on the trails?" She felt excitement coursing through her veins but also some apprehension. She hadn't forgotten her spill in the fall. "Do you think I'm good enough to be able to handle him?"

"Of course you are. You've got really good hands, Katie, and you've got a good feel for the horse. That's important. Plus, you're a lot lighter than I am. These Thoroughbreds are a thousand pounds of horseflesh sitting on top of little toothpick legs. That's why jockeys are so small; a big rider will break them down quicker."

There were a lot of good trails around the farms. They started out with King snubbed to the pony horse. Then when Katie was sure of herself and King, Jason undid the rope and they rode untethered beside his big Paint.

King was a joy to ride, but Katie had to continually be on her guard. Once while she was talking to Jason, she let her attention wander and a rabbit popped out from the bushes, startling King. The big colt jumped from the trail and ran a short distance before she was able to get him under control. Her heart hammered in her throat, and her hands were unsteady for quite a while, but she thought back to the lesson she had learned while swimming King in Mr. Simon's pool. She never went to sleep on the colt again.

*   *   *

The last week before King was to be sent to Willow Run, Katie and Jason were returning from their ride when she suggested they gallop across a big field. She had cantered King on the trail, but it hadn't been for very long, and she wanted to feel the pounding of his hooves and the wind in her hair one last time before she gave him over to John and another rider.

"I don't know if that's such a good idea, Katie," Jason said warily. "He's never had a big space like this to gallop in. We've kept him sandwiched in behind my horse all the time. He's starting to get fit, and he's feeling good."

"Come on, Jason," she begged. "Don't be a stick-in-the-mud. I won't let him go very fast."

She picked up a trot, then broke the colt into a slow canter. He had such a wonderfully long stride that he seemed to be eating the ground up beneath him.

Jason pulled along beside her. "Slow him down, Katie. You're going a little too fast."

She pulled back and King tossed his head, fighting for more rein. He was enjoying his run.

"Pull up!" Jason yelled to her over the pounding of hooves.

Katie stood in the stirrups for more leverage as she had seen the exercise riders do, but her stirrup irons were just too long. King took the bit in his teeth and bounded ahead of Jason's horse. His ears were pinned back against his head and his neck was stretched out before him. The trees and bushes passed by in a blur, and the cool spring wind stung her eyes, causing them to water.

She could hear Jason hollering in the background, but she was powerless to do anything but hang on and pray for a safe ride. If they hit a squirrel hole, King would probably break a leg. She didn't even want to think about that.

They had traveled about a half mile when she saw the fence looming ahead of them. She had to do something quickly, or they would crash right through it. Gathering her courage, she pulled at the bit in an easy, give-and-take motion. A solid tug had done no good. She remembered Jason telling her that racehorses were taught to run against the bit. "Easy, easy. Whoa, boy," she crooned over and over in a soothing voice, though her heart was racing as wildly as King's strides.

She saw the colt's ears flicker at the sound of her voice, and he began to respond to the pressure on his bit. The brain-numbing speed with which he had started his mad dash began to abate, and she felt she was regaining control. With only a hundred yards to go, King slowed to a manageable canter. Katie pulled him into a circle to the right, avoiding the four-board fence and bringing him to a halt.

Jason reached her a moment later. "Are you nuts!" he screamed as he jumped from his horse and ran to her. "You could have been killed!"

Katie slid from King's back. Her legs were so weak that they failed to support her, and she crumpled to the ground. Jason reached down to help her stand, supporting her with his arm about her waist. "Did you see how fast we went?" she said excitedly.

"How could I miss it—you left us in the dust."

Katie could tell Jason was irritated with her, but it didn't dampen her spirits. "We were racing the wind and we won!" Her voice was still shaking and her heart pounded so loudly she could hear it reverberating in her ears. She was shaken—never had she been on an animal that had moved so swiftly—but she was also ecstatic. "He can do it, Jason. King can win the big race."

Jason shook his head. "You're crazy, girl. You've just had a near brush with death, and all you can think about is a stupid horse race."

It was on the tip of her tongue to tell him that it wasn't a stupid horse race. A lot depended on King winning the Futurity. She was tired of seeing her mother work herself to exhaustion. But she clamped her mouth shut and looked at Jason—really looked at him. He was red in the face, and his hands were shaking as badly as hers. "You were worried about me," she said with wonder.

"Of course I was worried about you. Don't you know you could have been killed?"

Jason Roberts cared about her! What a day this had turned out to be. One moment she thought she was doomed, and the next minute she had a horse that was going to win the Futurity race and a guy who cared about her. Life was great. She gathered her soaring senses and calmed Jason down. Then they remounted their horses and walked back to the barn.

King was cooled out by the time they reached the stable. She drew a bucket of warm water and wiped the dried sweat from his coat, then walked him a bit more before turning him loose to graze. She would have to tell John about her wild ride. She hoped he wouldn't be angry with her. Most of all, she was worried that the run had hurt King's legs. If her unplanned sprint had hurt the colt, she would never forgive herself.

But King showed no sign of injury, so he was delivered to Willow Run as scheduled. John immediately set up a program. King's training would begin the following morning. Katie was up an extra hour early so she could help with the horses before going to school.

"Good morning, missy," John said cheerfully as he pulled the tack off the rail and entered King's stall. "You're here just in time."

"Do you need some help?" Katie entered the stall behind him and picked the saddle cloth and pad from the floor, brushing off the clinging straw. She put the cloth high up on King's withers, then slid it into place on his back, making sure all the hairs were smoothed in the right direction. Next came the pad, then the saddle.

"I've got a job for you if you think you can handle it," John said with a twinkle in his eye.

"What's that?" Katie was curious now. The old trainer looked as if he was up to something.

"Seems we've got an exercise rider who's out sick for a couple of days. Since you've been riding this colt, I thought you might like to start him on the track."

Katie's heart skipped a beat. "You mean like a *real* gallop boy?"

"That's right. I'll be ponying King for the first week, 'til he gets used to things. You're nearly old enough to get a license at the track. You might as well be learning along with this here colt. You're about the right size for the job. Go get a hard hat out of the tack room, and let's get to it."

Katie wanted to shout for joy. Never in her life had she imagined she would be able to ride on the big track. She had hinted to Mr. Ellis on several occasions, but he had always mumbled something about her not being strong enough. She knew it was just his polite way of saying he thought her handicap would prevent her from doing a good job. This was her chance to prove him wrong.

Katie ran to the carpeted tack room that housed all the riding equipment. There were several helmets hanging on the wall. She chose the one with red and blue stripes and fit it onto her head, hooking the chin strap into its catch. When she returned, John had King out in the shed row and was ready to go.

"First, we want to take these irons up a little higher than you've been used to. I'm going to teach you how to stand up in the irons and gallop racetrack style, but we don't want them too high yet, 'cause this colt isn't exactly one hundred percent broke."

Katie bent her leg and waited for John to give her a boost into the saddle. Since the stirrups were always so high, jockeys and exercise riders were given a leg up when mounting a horse.

It took her a few tries to get it right. She had to bounce a few times on her right leg, then use the pressure of the hand John had on her left leg to vault herself into the saddle. If she didn't have enough spring in her bounce, she couldn't get high enough in the air to get her leg over the saddle, but if she bounced too much, she could be thrown over the horse and land on the other side.

After a few tries, she finally got it right, and they headed out to the three-quarter-mile training track. The reins of the race bridle were different from any she had ever seen. There was rubber covering the ends the rider held. John said it was to keep the reins from slipping through her hands when she was working the horse.

When they reached the track, they entered the gate and rode clockwise at a walk on the outside rail.

"Always enter the gate clockwise, and backtrack at a walk or trot for a hundred yards or so," John instructed. "This keeps your horse calm and teaches him that he isn't going to jump right into the running as soon as he hits the track. That could cause an accident."

Several horses passed by at a gallop. King pranced and tossed his head, eager to be off. "Easy, boy." Katie settled him down.

"When it's time to turn around, always turn him toward the inner rail and make him stop for a second before you start. Take the time to walk him first, then break him into a trot, then a gallop. And always remember, the inside is for the faster-working horses. If you're just going to gallop like we're doing today, stay toward the center of the track."

They turned and stopped, then started King down the track.

Katie learned how to set the reins for maximum con-trol, so the horse was working more against himself than her arms, and how to stand in the stirrups with her body weight forward over the withers, the way the jockeys did. It was such an awkward position for her at first that her legs were exhausted by the time she finished the one-mile workout.

"Be here at the same time for the next couple of days, and we'll get you some more practice. Okay, Katie girl?"

"You bet! Oh, and, John, thanks for the chance." She turned to head back to her house. She had a half hour to get ready before the school bus came.

⇥ Chapter Twelve ⇤

For the next several days, Katie and King learned the workings of racetrack etiquette. Even after the other gallop boy came back to work, John continued to use her to exercise the colt.

"You're doing just fine," he assured her. "This colt is working real good for you, but we may have to put a stronger rider up when he starts getting racey. We can't have him running away with you." He looked up at Katie and smiled. "Guess you already know what that's all about."

She knew John was right, but she was still a little disappointed. Even though it had scared her, she had thrilled to every moment of their mad dash across the pasture. How much more fun it would be to pound around the smooth surface of the track with a clock to gauge their speed.

John noticed the frustrated look on her face and tried to soothe her injured feelings.

"Don't look so downcast, girl. I didn't say you'd never get to take him for a run. I just want to make sure that he doesn't start getting away from you when we want him to go slow. We don't need him hurting himself. It's hard enough to keep these horses together as it is."

As the days passed, Katie grew stronger and more sure of her capabilities. The other riders helped her as much as they could, and she was grateful to have such experienced people to work with.

Trouble struck on the first day of summer vacation. Cindy, who rarely made it out to the track so early in the morning, was standing at the rail when Katie pulled King up and walked him back to the exit gate.

"What are *you* doing out on the track?" Cindy accused. "Does my father know you're doing this?"

Cindy was always difficult, but ever since the horse show two years ago—and especially since she'd found out Jason had been spending so much time with Katie—Cindy had become even worse. She constantly found fault with Katie's work, even when there wasn't any, and she threatened to tell her father. Normally, Katie wouldn't have cared, but she needed the facilities to train King, and she enjoyed the company of the people she worked with.

"Daddy won't let me ride any of the racehorses, and you're not any older or better than I am. Why should you get to do it?" Cindy frowned and stood with her hands on her hips, glaring at her.

Katie was at a loss for words. She had assumed anything John wanted to do was okay with the stable owner. It never occurred to her that Mr. Ellis might not know that she had graduated from groom to exercise rider.

Now that she thought about it, they had been galloping King very early in the morning. Mr. Ellis usually showed up later to watch the older horses work out. He had never been there when she had come off the track.

John stepped forward and put a lead shank on King, walking him off the track. "You just run along now, Miss Ellis. I say Katie's riding this colt, and that's that."

"We'll see." Cindy turned in a huff and ran off toward the house.

"Are we in trouble, John? Can Cindy prevent me from riding Willow King?"

"She can try, but what it all boils down to is what's best for the horse. As long as you do well by this colt, Mr. Ellis won't have any reason to complain about you riding him." John waited for Katie to slip the bridle from King's head, then he put the halter on and buckled it.

"But he's *my* horse."

"That may be true, but this is *his* farm, and this colt is running under *his* stable name."

Katie felt like kicking something, most of all Cindy. Why didn't the girl just leave her alone and mind her own business? What did Cindy care if Katie got to ride on the track? The girl was such a poor rider, she would probably get somebody hurt if she was allowed to exercise the racehorses.

The next morning John surprised Katie by telling her that King was ready for his first timed workout and that she would be the rider aboard.

"We're only going to breeze him a quarter of a mile. I don't want him going full out," he instructed. "Back him up just a little bit, then gallop him around easy.

When you come up on the quarter pole, ease him over to the rail and cluck to him. Leave your whip here, 'cause I want him working on his own. I don't want you pushing him."

King must have felt her excitement because he chomped at the bit and pranced all the way to the track. "Easy, boy," she soothed. "We don't want you running off before it's time. You don't want to make me look bad, do you?"

As she rode King down the backstretch, she spotted a patch of yellow along the rail. Cindy was standing at the fence beside her father and John. The two men had their heads together and seemed to be in a heated argument. Cindy smiled sweetly and waved as Katie rode past.

Katie's heart dropped. Judging by the victorious grin on the brat's face, this would be the last chance she would have to ride King while he was in training. The colt felt the trembling in her hands and jerked at the bit.

"Not now, boy," she said as she brought the colt under control. "This time we're going to do it perfect."

When they approached the quarter pole, Katie looked over her shoulder to make sure there wasn't another rider coming up behind her, then eased King down next to the rail. She loosened her reins just a bit and clucked him into a faster stride. When she was fifteen yards from the red-and-white pole, she squatted into a jockey position and let King have his head, being careful to still keep a snug grip on the reins for support. The colt surged ahead, lengthening his stride as the dirt flew under his hooves. Katie felt the sting of his mane as it whipped against her face in a wild frenzy. They were flying!

All too soon, they passed the finish line. Katie stood up in the irons, letting King run a few more strides before she started to slow him from his blazing pace. If he were pulled up too quickly, he could seriously injure himself. She gently applied pressure on the bit, speaking softly to him, easing him back a little at a time. King acted as if he wanted to continue his run, but he responded to Katie's commands, slowing to a gallop, then pulling into a trot, then a walk.

"Good going, Katie," John said as he stepped up to grab King. The colt pranced off the racetrack, dragging John with him. "Whoa there, fella. No need to be getting headstrong just because you had a good workout."

"How'd he do?" Katie was excited, but she was also afraid to hear what Mr. Ellis might have to say.

"He worked in twenty-three and change," Mr. Ellis said. "Not bad for a colt's first breeze. That's better time than some of my older horses are working in." He looked to the trainer and nodded his head. "I think she'll do, John. Just keep going as you have been. If problems arise, we'll handle them when we come to them."

Katie sat up straighter on King and gave the stable owner a big smile. "I won't let you down, Mr. Ellis."

"I know you won't, Katie."

Cindy sulked behind her father. For once, she hadn't gotten her way. Katie waited until both the adults' heads were turned, then gave in to a childish urge. She turned to Cindy and stuck out her tongue, making a horrible face in the process. If Jason were here, he would call her a Stooge, but she didn't care; it felt good.

As the summer wore on, Katie didn't see much of Cindy, except when Jason was around, but she knew that Cindy wasn't done with her yet. Somewhere, her jealousy would raise its ugly head, and then there would be a price to pay.

King was to be shipped to Portland Downs racetrack in August, so he could be readied for the September meet. He had to have two officially timed workouts on record before he could start in his first race. John and Mr. Ellis also wanted to put a few races into the colt before the big Futurity.

Once at the track, King would be introduced to his new rider. Katie didn't have her gallop license yet, and no one was allowed on the track without a valid track identification. Besides, she would be in school then, and Portland was an hour away. She didn't have a license to drive a car either, so it would be impossible for her to get back and forth.

King worked well through the summer. He had grown in muscle and height, and he was moving well out of the starting gates. The only worry John had was for his legs. Most colts usually bucked their shins within the first sixty days of hard training.

"It's kind of like shin splints for an athlete," John explained. "They get a warm, painful swelling on the front of their cannon bone, and they have to be laid off for at least thirty days. Fortunately, it rarely ever happens to them twice."

One day as she was finishing up late, Katie heard footsteps coming up the shed row. The horses had been put to rest hours ago. It was unusual for someone to be in the barn at this time of night. One of the grooms always did a check around ten o'clock, but that was still an hour away.

She fastened King's bandage and stood to greet whoever was there. She rose just in time to see Cindy open the tack room door, looking in both directions before she quickly stepped inside.

Katie's curiosity was piqued. What was Cindy doing in the race barn? All of her tack was kept in the upper stable.

Katie ducked down to see through the crack in King's stall door. Cindy wouldn't be able to see her. Within a few minutes, Cindy emerged with a race bridle and one of the exercise saddles over her arm. She quickly closed the tack room door and hurried down the shed row.

Katie let herself out of King's stall and followed at a safe distance. She peeked around the corner and saw Cindy disappear into a stall halfway up the barn. A few minutes later, she led a horse out. It was Jester, and he was wearing the racetrack gear.

Katie pulled back quickly when Cindy mounted and turned Jester down the aisle. She ran back to King's stall and waited.

In a few moments, Cindy rode past. She had her irons raised to the height the exercise riders used, and she was trying–not very successfully–to stand in the stirrups the way the jockeys did.

What was she trying to prove? Katie wondered. Was she hoping to get good enough that her father would let her gallop his racehorses? The day that happened was the day Katie would stop riding at Willow Run. Cindy Ellis on horseback was an accident waiting to happen.

Her heart went out to Jester, but she told herself that the day was swiftly approaching when she would be able to get Jester back. She waited until Cindy and Jester turned the corner, then quickly let herself out of the barn.

As August came, John wanted to give King one last breeze before they sent him to the big track, so Katie was up early on a Saturday morning to ride. Jason had promised to stop by and watch the workout before he left for a cutting horse show in Portland. She hoped Cindy was staying in bed. It was always uncomfortable when the three of them were together.

On the way to King's barn, she stopped by to say hello to Jester and give him a treat, but he wasn't in his stall. She thought it odd but figured that with the nice weather he had been left out in the pasture overnight.

Jason was helping John tack up King when Katie arrived at the barn.

"Are you ready to set a new land speed record?" Jason teased.

John adjusted the pads and placed the saddle on King's back. "Don't be giving her any crazy ideas. I want a slow workout today." He tightened the girth, then signaled for Jason to give Katie a leg up.

Jason winked at her as he helped her onto the horse.

Katie could feel her cheeks burning. She felt giddy inside when he smiled at her like that.

"Good luck, Katie. Show 'em what you got." Jason gave her a thumbs-up sign.

"Thanks." She smiled and turned her concentration to King. This was an important day. She couldn't afford to divide her attention.

John gave her instructions on the way to the track.

"I want a nice, easy breeze for a half mile. Nothing fancy, just enough to leg him up for his official work at the big track." He stopped before they entered the gate. "Make sure he doesn't get away from you, girl. He's got some heat in those legs. We don't need him bucking his shins now. We need to get him in one of the first races, so we have a race date under our belt. If he wants to blow his shins after that, we can afford to give him a month off, but not now."

Katie nodded and gathered her reins. King had a nervous edge to him this morning. He pranced and threw his head around, straining at the bit. Each time a horse would race past him on the inside rail, he would jump, trying to get away from Katie so he could go with the other horse.

"Whoa, boy. What's eating you today? You ready to take on the world?"

She had to backtrack him an extra quarter mile to get him settled down, but when she turned and trotted him off, he seemed more relaxed. On her first pass down the back, she noticed Mr. Ellis standing by the outside rail. She smiled at him in the early morning light and held King to his steady pace.

As she galloped down the front stretch, with almost three furlongs to go before she hit the half-mile pole, King flicked his ears and threw his head in the air, trying to snatch the bit from her grip. "What the...?" Katie muttered to herself as she knuckled him back under control and looked about for the cause of his spooking. A moment later she heard a loud cry and looked over her right shoulder to see Cindy on horseback, swooping down upon them.

As Cindy flew past on the outside rail, spurring her horse, Katie noticed with horror that the poor beast was Jester. The only resemblance the animal bore to her once-beloved horse was the white star on his forehead. Everything else about him had a wild look. His eyes were rolling back and forth so the whites showed, and he was drenched in sweat from head to hoof. White foam flecked from his mouth and blew on them as he passed.

"Catch us if you can, slowpokes," Cindy yelled as she flew past them.

King wasn't used to having a fast-working horse approach him from the outside, and the screaming and pounding of hooves spooked him out of his calmness. He tossed his head in the air again and again until he almost unseated Katie, then he grabbed the bit and surged ahead, trying to catch Jester.

Katie stood in the irons and pulled with all her might, but it wasn't enough to slow the colt. King flattened his ears against his head and ran full out, his legs pumping like pistons, until he caught up to Cindy. Jester was no racehorse; he knew when he was beaten and he tried to lessen his pace, but Cindy drew her whip and flogged him.

King leaped ahead and continued to open the distance between them. This was the first time he had ever raced against another horse and he was in his glory.

This couldn't be happening. It was like a bad dream that she couldn't wake from. Katie continued to stand in the stirrups. She was going faster than she ever had aboard a horse. If she hadn't been so miserable, she might have enjoyed it, but she knew what the fast pace would do to King's legs. Especially over the distance they were traveling.

Jester finally dropped out, making it easier for her to slow King down. By the time she broke his pace, he had traveled a mile at the wretchedly fast clip. She pulled him up on the back side of the track. King took several faltering steps. By the time they reached the exit gate, the colt was limping so badly that she had to dismount.

Tears streamed down her face, but she didn't have any more control over them than she had over King's wild workout.

Jason grabbed the reins and quieted King, while John pulled the saddle off.

"It wasn't your fault, Katie girl. You did everything you could," John assured her.

She could barely talk for the tears choking her throat. "It doesn't matter whose fault it was, John. King is injured, and now we're not going to be able to get him in an early race. How could Cindy do such a thing? Where is she?" Katie turned, looking frantically around the stable area.

"I can't believe she would do such a stupid thing," Jason said. "I'm going to have a talk with her. She can't get away with this."

"Just settle down," John ordered. "I suspect her father will handle this. By the look in his eyes, I wouldn't want to be in her shoes right now."

Katie turned to see Cindy being grabbed from Jester's back by Mr. Ellis. John was right: he looked like a bull ready to charge a red cape.

"Come on. We've got to get this colt taken care of," John said. "Jason, run on ahead and get the hot water ready for King's bath. And, Katie, you prepare his stall."

"Excuse me, John." The timid voice of a stable boy who usually did the clocking cut in. "I thought you might be interested...I caught the colt going a mile in a minute and thirty-eight seconds."

John's brows shot up and he looked back at the boy. "Keep that under your hat, okay? I don't want anyone but me and Mr. Ellis to know. Not even any of the help, understand?"

"Yes, sir." The boy went back to his job.

"Is that good?" Katie asked the trainer.

"For this track, and under those conditions, I'd say it was more than good. Don't you go worryin' none about that Futurity, little gal. This is just a minor setback. We're going to get there, you mark my words. Now, run along and ready that stall."

⇌ Chapter Thirteen ⇌

King spent the next thirty days recovering from his injury. He was turned out in a small pasture by himself for the first couple of weeks. Moving was painful, and he hobbled from one patch of grass to another.

Katie's heart went out to him. She remembered when she was younger and she had been put in a partial body cast to correct a problem her short leg had caused with her back. She had been so sore, and moving had been very painful.

Jan climbed onto the fence next to her, breaking her reverie.

"He looks like he's walking on eggshells," Jan observed.

"He's really hurting," Katie agreed. "It took me almost a half hour to walk him to this pasture, and it's only a couple of hundred yards from the barn. The poor guy almost fell down several times."

"What happened to Cindy?" Jan asked. "After all the damage she's done, I hope her father grounded her for life."

Katie frowned. "I don't even want to hear her name. I heard some of the stable hands talking. They said that she's grounded to the house for a couple of weeks, and she's restricted from the stable area for a month. If it wasn't for Cindy's stupid trick, King could have won his first race by now."

At the mention of his name, Willow King raised his elegant head and nickered, staring thoughtfully at Katie as he chewed on a mouthful of the tender grass.

"See? He thinks so, too." Katie jumped down from the fence and offered King an apple. He stretched his neck to receive the treat, then munched happily while Katie petted his neck.

"You told me that John says he'll be walking better pretty soon," Jan said. "This horse sure has a lot of heart. He faces all kinds of adversity and just keeps going."

"Yeah," Katie said as she scratched him behind the ears. "I should take some lessons from him. He's a lot braver than I am," she said, thinking of the one and only time a boy had asked her to dance, and what a fool she'd made of herself. Katie wondered if she'd ever get another chance to dance with Jason—and whether she'd have the nerve to try it again if he ever did ask her. But after the way she had behaved, she sincerely doubted that he would ever ask her again.

"You're a lot braver than you think you are, Katie. You've got real inner strength."

Katie shrugged off the compliment. She wished she had as much confidence in herself as Jan had. "Anyway, King won't be ready to train until his thirty days are up. He won't have enough time to get ready for the big race." Katie kicked at a big lump of dirt. "It's so unfair! By the time King's stood around for a month, he'll have lost a lot of the endurance we've helped him gain."

"Maybe not." Jan hopped off the fence and came to stand in front of Katie.

"What do you mean?"

King paused in his grazing as if he, too, were interested in what Jan had to say.

"Remember Mr. Simon and his horse pool? A lot of the horses he was swimming were broken-down horses that couldn't take the pounding on the racetrack."

Katie brightened. "You're right. He said that swimming kept their wind built up while they were healing. I bet that King will be walking well enough in a week that we could take him out to the pool and start swimming him again."

"I'll call Mr. Simon tonight," Jan offered.

"Thanks, pal. You might have just saved King's career."

By September, when King should have been racing, he was just starting back into training at the track. But thanks to the horse pool, he bounced back quickly, and they were able to enter him in a race much sooner than they had originally anticipated.

School had started. Katie was in eleventh grade now, and the homework was tougher than ever, but with King's race coming up, she just couldn't keep her mind on the tasks at hand. When the bell rang, ending the school week, she dashed home and quickly packed her suitcase. Her mother had agreed to drive her and Jan to

Portland that night. King didn't race until two o'clock the next afternoon, but Katie wanted to spend as much time with him as possible. Jason would drive up and meet them a couple of hours before the race.

Katie was a nervous wreck the next morning. She woke feeling sick to her stomach, so she ate a light breakfast and hurried to the track.

"You look like an old mother hen," John said as he watched her fuss over King. "If you keep brushing that horse, he's not going to have any hide left."

"But I want him to look pretty," she protested.

"All horses look good when they're in the winner's circle." He chuckled. "Come on, now, get on out of there. You're making me nervous just watchin' you. We don't need to get this colt worked up before his race."

Katie gave King a pat, and he nuzzled her pocket looking for a treat. "Sorry, boy, you know the rules. No food until after your race. We don't want you getting a stomachache while you're running." She straightened his forelock and looked into his brown eyes. "But I've got a bag of carrots in the tack room. They're all yours if you do well."

A half hour before the race, they started preparing King. His hooves were picked, and he was brushed again until he gleamed. Katie brought blue carnations to weave into his mane and tail. They matched the color of silks the jockey would wear. Blue was her favorite color— it was a good sign.

"Do you think we've got a chance to win this one, John?" Katie asked as she fumbled nervously with the mane and tail comb.

"Every horse in this race has a chance to win it. That's horse racing." He flipped through the pages of *The Daily Racing Form.* "The biggest competition will be that colt Raging Wind. They're priming him for the Kentucky Derby."

Katie's stomach flopped. Did they stand a chance against a Derby horse?

John folded the paper and put it in his hip pocket. "Don't go looking so worried, Katie girl. We've got as good a shot as he does to win this race. King's every bit as good as Raging Wind–maybe a little better."

Katie smiled. John was right. King was a champion, and today he was going to prove it.

"You got your new license?" John asked.

She nodded.

"Make sure you keep it on you, 'cause they'll probably ask for it."

Mrs. Durham, along with Jan and Jason, stopped by to wish them luck before going over to the grandstand. "Mr. Ellis said he would be in the paddock if you needed any help saddling," Katie's mother said. "We'll meet you over there."

Jason stepped forward and took her hand, giving it a gentle squeeze. "Good luck, Katie. I'll be waiting for you on the front side."

Katie blushed furiously. When Jason looked at her like that, it made her feel as if she had a thousand butterflies whirling in her stomach.

When the call to the gate came, they bridled King and flushed his mouth with cool water, then took him out to stand in the shed row.

"Keep him here until the gate pops on the race before King's. I don't want him getting excited when he hears those other horses running down the backstretch. I'll holler when it's time to bring him for his race. You all right, girl? You look a little pale."

"I'm fine, John. Just a little nervous."

John laughed. "You better get used to it. This colt's got a lot of races in him."

King sensed her nervousness and began to fidget. She put a hand on either side of his bit and gently shook it, just as John had showed her. The colt became interested in the game and forgot his dancing around.

Katie listened to the sound of the announcer as he called the loading of the gate. It was a six-furlong race—three-quarters of a mile—so the starting gate was on the backstretch. She was close enough to hear the doors slam and the gate men yelling directions to one another as they loaded the nervous animals. When the last one was in, she heard the starter say, "Everyone get tied on." Then the bell rang and the doors clanged open. The pounding of hooves echoed up and down the barns.

King jumped when he heard the commotion, lifting his tail in the air and blowing a great gust of air through his nostrils.

"Whoa, boy. Save your energy for your race." She heard John call, so she led King out, handing him to the man on the pony horse who was to take him to the front. She cut across the infield with John.

The paddock area, where the horses were saddled, contained twelve stalls, each painted in a different color. John took King from the pony horse's rider and brought him into the saddling stall. They had drawn the number-two post, so they would be one of the first to be tacked.

When all the equipment was in place, Katie took King out to walk around the circle. This helped loosen him up, and also gave the public an opportunity to see what they were betting on. As they made their rounds, she heard lots of oohs and aahs. Katie smiled proudly and patted King on the neck.

"Bring 'em in," the paddock judge yelled. Because it was King's first race, the official had to check King's tattoo and body markings against the registration papers to make sure the right horse was racing. He grabbed King's lip and rolled it back, reading the smudged blue-black numbers and letters. When he was satisfied that they were correct, he compared King's markings with those described on the papers. He walked behind King and brushed at the small patch of white on his right heel.

"This white isn't listed," he said as he stood and surveyed the paperwork again.

"Let me see that." John took the papers from him and a frown furrowed his brow.

Katie didn't like the look on either man's face. "What's that mean?" she asked with rising panic.

John turned to her and shook his head. "It means they can scratch the horse," he said.

"No," she whispered, afraid that if she said it any louder, it would come out a scream. "We've come so far, how can something as simple as a few white hairs stop us?"

"It's the racing rules," the paddock judge offered. "But I'll tell you what I'm going to do. Everything else checks out. I'll let you run him today, but you'll have to get these papers fixed before you race him again. Contact the jockey club tomorrow, and they'll take care of it."

"Thank you!" Katie gave him her best smile.

King entered the track to the sound of the trumpet calling the horses to the post. They paraded at a walk in front of the audience, then trotted or galloped back to the gate. Her mother and friends sat up in the clubhouse with Mr. Ellis, but Katie preferred to stand next to the fence with John.

The first horse was loaded into the gate. Katie's nerves were stretched so tightly that she thought she would burst. King stood behind the gate, and she held her breath, praying that he wouldn't give the loaders any trouble. He stepped into the number-two hole, and Katie let out her breath—then held it again in anticipation of the start.

"They're off!" the announcer yelled into the microphone.

From where she stood, Katie could see King striving to take the lead. Two other horses were running with him, the rest of them trailing behind.

"It's Raging Wind in the lead, with Simple Lad and Willow King running neck and neck behind him," the man with the microphone announced.

"Get him out of there, Randy!" John instructed the jockey, as if he could hear him. "He's trapped on the rail. He's got no place to run."

Katie watched as King held his ground, neither able to pass the leader nor draw to the outside. She knew Randy was doing his best. He had been the Ellis farm's jockey for many years. He had worked King several times and was familiar with the colt. Before the race, he had told Katie they had a good shot at winning.

Katie lost sight of King as the leading horses went into the turn and the rest of the pack caught up to them.

"He's got to do something now," John said. "Get him out of that hole!"

Katie's heart sank as she saw the blue colors fade back into the pack. What had happened? Had King run out of breath? Were his legs hurting again?

The announcer broke in. "Willow King seems to be having some difficulty. He's fading fast, and Usurper has moved up to battle for the lead."

Katie put her forehead on the cool metal of the fence. She couldn't bear to watch. All her hopes were being crushed beneath the pounding hooves of the racing horses.

"Here he comes!" John jarred her arm, then slapped his hands on the fence. "Come on, King!" he screamed.

"Willow King is making a comeback on the outside," the announcer said. "Look at him run! He's passed Usurper and is moving up to challenge the leader, Raging Wind."

Katie's head snapped up. She could see a patch of blue coming on the outside. "You can do it, King!" she screamed with all her might. She jumped onto the cement ledge the fence rested on and strained her eyes to see what was happening.

The pounding of hooves as the horses entered the homestretch and the roar of the crowd was deafening. She could see King on the outside of the pack, but from her angle, she couldn't tell if he was running first or second.

"It's Raging Wind and Willow King coming down to the wire....Raging Wind and Willow King..." The announcer paused for emphasis. "And at the finish line, it's Willow King by a nose!"

Suddenly, Katie's mother, Jan, Jason, and Mr. Ellis were surrounding her and John, patting them both on their backs and shouting congratulations. Jason picked her up and swung her in a circle. In the midst of all the commotion, she looked up to see a man staring at her and frowning heavily. He quickly walked away. Katie turned back to her friends, not giving the strange man another thought.

"Here he comes, Katie."

As King trotted back to the winner's circle, his sides were heaving and sweat dripped from his body. He held his head proudly and looked every bit the winner he was.

"Grab him and lead him into the winner's circle while I get everyone herded into there," John instructed.

They posed for the win photo, and Katie was sure that all they would be able to see of her would be a big set of teeth. She was smiling so hard, her face hurt. After the picture was taken, she waited for the jockey to undo King's saddle. She noticed the man who had given her a dirty look talking to the jockey of Raging Wind. He still didn't look very happy. After a short discussion, he took the second-place horse by the reins and led him back to the stable. Katie quickly put him out of her mind. She had a winner to cool down and a celebration to start.

Now was not the time for dark thoughts.

Jason met her at the barn with a bucket of warm water and King's cooling-out blanket. "John says we've got to go to the test barn. Grab King's halter and let's go. We'll bathe him there."

Katie picked up the halter and lead rope and followed Jason to the test barn. This was where the horses were tested to make sure they ran legally, without any drugs in their systems.

Katie and Jason showed their identification to the guard at the gate, then entered the area. The afternoon was cooling down and steam rose from the colt's sweat-soaked body. In the distance, the bugle sounded, calling the horses to the post for the next race. Tired as he was, King pricked his ears and listened, then pawed the ground and snorted.

"Looks like he's ready to go again!" Jason said.

Katie laughed as she dunked the sponge into the warm water and squeezed it over King's coat. "He may be ready to go again, but I don't think I could handle the pressure. I was so nervous during the race. When he ran into trouble on the last turn, I about died! I'm glad we've got another couple of weeks before we have to do this again."

Jason patted her shoulder. "You better get used to it, kid. I think we'll be doing a lot more of this in the future. How about if we all go out for pizza tonight to celebrate the win? I'm buying."

"That would be great. I'll ask my mom and Jan."

A radio played in the background and the chords of Jason's favorite song drifted across the test barn. He looked at her, but she immediately turned away, reaching for the scraper to remove the excess water from King's coat. She despised herself for being such a chicken. She knew the dance. There was nobody watching. What was her problem?

"You know you owe me a dance?" Jason said.

"I know," she said quietly. "And someday I'll do it, just not now. You know…with King and all…"

"That's okay, Katie. I'm a patient guy. And my foot's almost healed…" he teased.

Katie laughed and prepared to throw the sponge at him, but the smile froze on her face. Standing just past Jason's shoulder outside the test barn stood the tall man with the beady eyes who had given her such a sour look.

"What's the matter, Katie? You look like you saw a ghost." He turned to look at the barn opposite the test area, but there was no one there.

"It's nothing," she said as she forced a smile to her lips. It was probably all in her imagination. The man just had an unpleasant face, and it only seemed like he was glaring at her. She put him out of her mind. "Let's talk about that pizza."

⇥ *Chapter Fourteen* ⇤

The next morning, King was clamoring for his breakfast.

"That's a good sign," John said. "The race didn't take too much out of him or he'd be off his feed."

Katie mixed the grain while King bobbed his head and nickered, pawing at the ground for emphasis. "I think he would like to eat his food and everyone else's, too." She laughed as she dumped the grain into his bucket. "So when exactly does he race next?"

"Patience, missy. I don't like running these young horses any closer than three or four weeks apart, but the Futurity is only a month away, and I'd like to get one more start into him before then. I guess two weeks from now would be a good time."

"Is he coming home tomorrow?"

Old John tipped his hat back on his head. "I've been thinking on that. The colt's been doing pretty good here. I hate hauling them back and forth if it's not necessary. He's your horse, but my advice is to leave him here at the track. I can bring you up with me on the weekends if you like."

"That's fine. I trust your judgment. At least I'll get to see him on the weekend. Jason's offered to drive me, too." At John's smirk, she blushed. "He's just a friend." She quickly changed the subject. "Who's that guy?" She pointed at a tall figure across the barn. It was the same man who had stared so angrily at her the night before.

"That's the trainer of Raging Wind."

"The horse we beat yesterday?"

"Yes. The man's name is Orlin Caldwell. He's also the colt's owner. He's not too happy with us today. He'd been bragging around that his colt couldn't be beat. He's got Derby plans for that horse, and it doesn't look good for him to get beat by a colt that's come out of the blue."

"He gave me a dirty look yesterday," she said.

"Better steer clear of that one, Katie girl. He's a bad seed. He was ruled off the track for a year. They caught him doping his horse before a race. It's too bad the likes of him has got his hands on such a nice colt."

The two weeks before King's next race passed in a blur. Soon, Jason was picking her and her mother up for the drive to Portland. When they arrived, it was still early, but already the track was a hive of activity.

John handed her the grooming tools as soon as she walked down the shed row. "You might as well go see if you can scrub the rest of the hair off him," he teased.

Jason held King while she ran the rubber curry over his body. He twitched and acted as if he wanted to nip her, but he knew better. When she was done with the curry, she threw it into his feed pail, intending to start with the soft brush, but her attention was drawn to the bucket.

"Look at this," she said as she tipped the bucket so Jason could see. "He's got a lot of grain left here. Call John and ask him if he gave King some extra grain."

When the old trainer stepped into the stall, he examined the contents of the bucket. "King cleaned up his grain this morning. Someone's put this here since then."

"This may not be a nice thing to say, but has Cindy been here?" Katie asked.

"No, I think her dad's grounded her for life," Jason said.

John inspected the grain a little closer, rolling the oats around in his palm. "Why, look here! See this white stuff?"

Katie saw the small chunks of white. It reminded her of aspirin. John put one of the pieces to his tongue and made a face at the taste of it.

"It's bute. Someone's slipped this horse some bute."

"You mean the painkiller?" Jason asked.

"Yes, and in Oregon, it's illegal to run a horse on that medication unless the track vet has put the horse on the bute list. King isn't on that list."

"What do we do now?" Katie asked.

John wiped his hands on his trousers and shook his head. "We don't know if King's eaten any of this or not. We'll have to report it to the track stewards and scratch him from the race."

"Scratch him? But there's not another race we can get him in before the Futurity!" Katie exclaimed.

"I know that, missy, but we can't take the chance. If he wins the race, we'll have to go to the test barn. If the bute shows up in his urine, they'll take the purse away. And I'll lose my license. We don't know for sure if he's eaten any of this. We can't take that chance."

"But why would somebody do this?" Katie could feel tears burning the backs of her eyes.

"It looks like somebody didn't want this horse to win. They probably figured King would eat all of the food— and we'd have a bad test and get the race taken away from us. Either that, or they counted on us pulling out of the race," John said. "Looks like they got their wish."

Two hours later, after reporting the incident to the track authorities for investigation, they sat in the stands and watched Raging Wind win King's race by six lengths.

"We could have beat him again," Katie said. "King ran a much faster time."

"Sorry to hear about your horse, John," Orlin Caldwell said after walking his horse from the winner's circle.

"I just bet you are," Katie muttered under her breath. But she had no proof that Orlin Caldwell was to blame for the bute, only a gut feeling.

That night, they shipped King back to Willow Run Farm. He wasn't safe at the track anymore. Katie was glad to have him home. Because of the missed race, King would have to work extra hard to get in shape for the one-mile Futurity.

*   *   *

The Saturday before the big race, Katie got up before sunrise to help John feed. She got there a few minutes ahead of the trainer, so she measured out the grain for each horse, then grabbed a carrot to slip King before the morning feed. Each horse poked his head over the stall door and nickered to her as she passed.

King's stall was quiet when she got to it. Was it possible he was still sleeping? She opened the door and saw his dark shape lying in the middle of the stall. "Time to get up, you lazy bum." As she reached for the light switch, a pain-filled groan came from the horse. Katie rushed to King's side and knelt in the straw. She reached out to touch his coat and cringed when she felt the cold sweat covering his body. She jumped up and quickly turned on the light.

The pale electric bulb penetrated the dark corners of the box stall, revealing signs of a struggle. The stall was in total disarray from where King had pawed the floor, mixing the dank earth with his straw bedding. He had obviously rolled many times, and the mixture of dirt and straw clung to his wet coat. In the corner, a partial flake of extremely moldy alfalfa lay beneath some half-eaten grass hay.

King pulled his head around, trying to nip at his sides, then tucked his legs and attempted to roll again. Colic! Willow King had colic!

Katie ran from the barn and sped to John's little house at the edge of the stable yard. A light was on in his kitchen. She pounded frantically at the door until he answered.

"Katie...?"

"Call the vet, John! King has colic really bad!"

"Throw a light blanket on him and get him up and walking. Don't let him roll, or he could twist a gut and we'll lose him," John ordered as he grabbed the phone. "Let's hope we're not too late. I'll be there as soon as I can."

Katie's heart was in her throat. *Lose him.* She prayed they were not too late. Grabbing a halter from the tack room, she ran to King's stall and fastened it on his head. "Come on, boy. You've got to get up." She tugged on the rope, but King refused to budge. He uttered a groan and tried to roll again.

"No!" she screamed as she took the end of the lead rope and brought it down hard against his flank. She had never whipped King before, but now it seemed the only way to save his life. "Get up!" she hollered and slapped the rope across his hindquarters. That got his attention, and he scrambled to get to his feet. "Attaboy," she encouraged him as he stood and swayed. "Good boy, King."

She opened the stall door and pulled him into the shed row. The sun was coming up, and the early morning light showed the pain etched on King's noble face. "You'll be okay," she crooned as they walked slowly down the way.

The stable's grooms trickled in one by one, and word spread quickly that the colt was ill. The veterinarian arrived within twenty minutes and immediately set to work on the colicky horse.

"Will he be all right?" Katie asked as Dr. Marvin put the stethoscope to King's belly.

"There's a lot of rumbling in there, but it sounds like his intestines are functioning. I don't think anything's been twisted. I'm going to give him something to relax him, then run a little bit of oil into his gut to see if we can't get rid of that bad hay. He should be back to normal in a day or two."

She heaved a sigh of relief. King was going to be okay.

John came out of King's stall with the half-eaten flake of moldy hay. "Did you bring this from home, Katie?"

"No, I thought somebody from here must have accidentally fed it to him."

"This was no accident. All our hay goes in the hay nets. This flake was on the ground, and it's not even the same kind of alfalfa we use. See here? Look at how big the stems are. Our hay is a lot finer."

"You mean somebody came on this property and purposely fed King bad hay?" She sat down hard on a bale of straw, the implication of what John said sinking into her confused brain. "What about Cindy? Could she have done it?"

"Not likely. The whole family's gone this weekend." John tossed the bad hay into the trash can. "Last week it was bute, now moldy hay. I'd say someone on the outside doesn't want us running this colt."

"So what do we do?" At the moment, she felt so helpless.

"First, we see how this colt bounces back. This is

going to cost us a couple of days of training, and that's not good. When he's ready to train again, we've got to decide if we're going to run him or if we're going to knuckle under to this type of dirty work."

"Who would do such a thing?" she asked, but already a picture of the tall man with the angry face loomed in her mind. She looked at John and knew he was thinking the same thing. Katie stood with hands on hips, her mouth set in a determined line. "I say we fight this thing!"

"I was hoping you would say that." John smiled and slapped her on the shoulder. "Call Jason and Jan and see if they'll help. We're going to have to set up watches around the clock. I don't want this colt left alone for one minute. No one relaxes until we've won the Futurity!"

⊰ Chapter Fifteen ⊱

"I can't believe anyone could stoop so low!" Jason grumbled as he ran his hand over King's sleek coat. "He could have killed this colt."

"We're not sure it was Orlin," Katie said, but it was a weak protest. She was almost positive it was the creepy trainer of Raging Wind.

"Who else could it be? King's his main competition," Jason argued. "I mean, sure, there're some other nice colts here, but King is the toughest competition for Raging Wind. If King's out of the way, Caldwell's colt will have a much easier time winning the Futurity."

Katie nodded. "I just wish we had some proof, but John says Orlin is too smart for that. The only thing we can do is keep an eye on King around the clock."

"Well, you can count on me." Jason grabbed his sleeping bag and threw it into the tack room. "You and Jan can split the day shift, and John and I will take the night watch."

"Thanks, Jason." Katie smiled at him. "You've been a real friend. I don't know what King and I would have done without you."

Jason winked and gave her a brilliant smile. "I'm glad you didn't have to find out." He reached out and brushed a stray lock of hair from Katie's face. "You're special, Katie Durham. I'm glad we're friends."

Race day arrived and Katie woke with the feeling of internal butterflies. True to Dr. Marvin's prediction, King had been back to his normal self in a couple of days and had been eager to train. They had pushed him hard to ready him for the grueling race, but John still worried that the horse might not be fit enough to compete in top form.

Another worry was the lineup of horses for the race. Orlin Caldwell had two horses running in the Futurity. Although Raging Wind was going to be tough to beat, the other horse didn't even belong in the race.

"He's just a cheap claimer that Orlin's put in to give us trouble," John said. "He drew the hole next to ours. If he boxes us in, we're going to be hurtin'."

At first Caldwell had seemed surprised to see King back at the track. But he smiled his oily smile at Katie and went back to work. She couldn't prove he had sabotaged King. The only way to get her revenge was to beat him fair and square.

A half hour before the call to the gate, Katie entered King's stall and set to work. "You're going to look like royalty," she said as she wove purple ribbons and carnations into his mane and tail.

"You're going to make him look like a sissy," Jason teased from outside the stall.

"You hush," Katie replied. "I want him to look beautiful for the win picture." She picked out his hooves and brushed his coat until it gleamed in the sunlight. This was only King's second race, but by now he had figured out what was happening, and he fidgeted, eager to be on with the business at hand.

They announced the call to the paddock. Katie waited for John's signal before she led King out to the pony horse. Orlin Caldwell walked by with Raging Wind and tipped his hat in their direction, a mischievous smile playing about his lips.

"Good luck, folks. May the best horse win." He laughed and walked on.

"Don't let him get to you," Jason said as he stepped up to grab her hand and give it a squeeze. "You've got the best horse, and he knows it. He wouldn't dare try anything in the race."

"Don't be so sure of that," John cautioned. "But, whatever he does, we'll be ready for him. I've already talked to our jockey. He knows to be on the lookout for trouble."

King pranced about the paddock, showing off for the public. In the post parade, he bowed his neck and strutted. The people remembered him from his last performance, and the odds on King dropped dramatically.

"Looks like the public has picked him to win," Jason said as he came to stand beside her. "Come on. We're supposed to meet everybody up in the Turf Club. John wants to watch the race from up there."

Katie climbed the stairs two at a time. Her heart was beating in triple time. She reached Mr. Ellis's reserved table just as the horses were being loaded into the gate. Her mother reached over and patted her arm.

"Quit shaking, dear. Everything's going to be fine," Mrs. Durham said.

Katie smiled and gave her a hug. "I hope so. This is what we've been waiting for, Mom." She laughed nervously. An awful lot depended on this race. Her mom had been working so hard to keep the farm's taxes paid. And Katie herself had given up Jester for so long. All for this one moment.

Katie truly believed that King was a champion. She'd believed in him from the first moment she'd laid eyes on him, even with those pitifully deformed legs. No one but Katie had been able to see into his heart and spirit. No one else had wanted to give him a chance.

For Katie, the winning wasn't really about the money. In her heart, she knew it was about something much more important. King *had* to win!

She spotted Mr. Caldwell sitting several tables down from her and resisted the urge to make a face at him.

"The last horse is being loaded in the gate for this year's running of the Portland Downs Futurity," the track announcer called.

"And they're off!"

King broke from his outside post position and dropped down to the inner part of the track. High Tide, the weaker half of the Caldwell entry, was on the inside rail, running next to him.

"That's good," John said. "At least we're not trapped on the rail with no place to run."

Raging Wind had taken the lead, and King was running fifth, next to High Tide. "How come he's so far back?" Katie asked.

"He's sitting just where I want him," John replied. "With that missed race, this colt's not fit enough to go out there on the engine and set blistering fractions. Let Caldwell's horse do that, and when he tires, we'll catch him in the homestretch."

The horses thundered down the backstretch, and King moved up in position, gaining on the lead horse with each stride of his powerful legs.

"That's it, King!" Katie shouted as he moved into third place. Her adrenaline was pumping so hard that she felt she was going to faint.

"Raging Wind is hanging on to his lead. Flaggstaff and Willow King have moved up to challenge as they enter the last turn on the way to the homestretch." The announcer's voice boomed throughout the building.

"High Tide is now moving on the inside, coming up to challenge Willow King!"

A sudden intake of breath from the crowd alerted Katie that something had gone wrong. She stood on tiptoe to see what had happened.

"High Tide has blown the turn and is taking Willow King to the outside rail with him. It looks like it's all over for these two colts. Raging Wind is still in the lead as they come out of the turn and head down the homestretch!"

"No!" Katie shouted as she bolted into the aisle for a better view. King's jockey was standing in the irons, trying to slow his horse enough to duck in behind the drifting Caldwell horse. Katie gasped as King appeared to trip over the other colt's hind legs, but he righted himself and surged back into the race, his long stride eating up the ground beneath him. He had already lost many lengths on the other horses, but his heart wouldn't let him quit.

"Ladies and gentlemen, Willow King has freed himself from the tangle and is back in the race!" the voice from the microphone blared.

"Look at him go!" Katie jumped up and down and pounded on Jason's back. "Here he comes!"

The crowd went wild as Willow King made a valiant effort to catch the leader. He roared down the homestretch, nostrils flaring and hooves churning the dirt. With a sixteenth of a mile to go, he caught Raging Wind, and the two horses ran neck and neck to the finish line.

"It's a photo finish!" the announcer said. "Hold all tickets for the results."

Katie ran down the stairs, pushing past Orlin Caldwell at the door.

"Watch it, little girl," he growled menacingly. "You wouldn't want to get hurt."

Katie turned to face him. "I'm not afraid of you." She squared her shoulders and lifted her chin. "I know that was no accident out there on the last turn. You don't deserve to win this race. You don't deserve a horse as good as Raging Wind!" She turned and bolted out the door, running to catch Willow King.

King trotted back to the winner's circle. The jockey removed his goggles and spoke to them. "It was so close, I'm not even sure who got it. Regardless of who wins, this is one fine horse. He gave it everything he had."

Both riders of the photo-finish horses stayed in the saddle, circling their mounts as they waited for the results. The neon sign that announced the inquiry went out, and a murmur arose from the crowd as they waited for the winner's number to be posted on the board. The number nine was put first, and King's jockey stood in the stirrups, his crop held victoriously over his head in a salute.

"We did it!" Jason grabbed her and whirled her around in a circle. "King won the Futurity!"

"We won!" she whispered in awe, then jumped up and down, clapping her hands together. "We really, really won!"

John grabbed King as Katie herded everyone into the winner's circle. She felt like she was in a dream. One week ago she thought King was going to die, and now she stood posing in the winner's circle after the Portland Downs Futurity.

Everyone chattered excitedly as they walked back to the barn, shaking hands and thumping one another on the back. King tossed his head and stepped proudly. Several hundred yards ahead of them, Katie could see Orlin Caldwell leading Raging Wind back to his stall.

"Katie girl, you take King to the test barn. I'll send Jason down with his halter and water bucket," John said.

She took King and walked to the fenced-in barn, wondering if Raging Wind would be required to give a urine sample. Sometimes they only tested the first-place horse; other times they took the first three. She hoped King would be the only one this time. She didn't want to see that tall creepy man again. Now that they had won the Futurity, she hoped that he would leave them alone.

Katie looked up when she heard a car driving down the pavement that separated the barns. It was unusual for there to be a vehicle on the grounds during the races. Only the veterinarians were allowed to have their cars inside the gates at race time. But this was a police car.

John arrived at the same time as Jason. They showed their identification at the test barn gate, then entered the enclosure.

"Justice is served!" John said as he picked up the hose and ran the water over King's steaming body. "They've arrested Orlin for allegedly conspiring to tamper with a race."

"But how? I know he did it, but we've got no proof." Katie was dumbfounded.

"Seems he promised that jockey aboard High Tide a piece of the action if he knocked King out of the race. Since we won, Orlin refused to give him a dime. The track stewards were a little suspicious of the race and called that rider to their office to question him. The poor kid got scared and told them everything he knew in return for leniency. Caldwell is busted. I think this will finish his career as a trainer."

"But what about Raging Wind? He's such a good horse. It's too bad his career has ended too."

"Oh, I wouldn't worry about that. Caldwell's no

dummy. Even if he goes to jail, he'll either sell the colt or put him in someone else's name. We'll meet up with him again," John said as he took the metal scraper and wiped the extra water from King's coat.

"What about the Derby?" she asked hesitantly.

"What Derby?" John said with a knowing smile. "You mean the Kentucky Derby? What about it?"

"Do you think we have a chance at it? Raging Wind was headed to the Derby, and we've beat him twice. The race today was only a couple of tenths off the track record. If King could almost fall down and still come within a hair of the record, I'd say that was pretty good."

"But Raging Wind was nominated into that race. You have to pay a lot of money to get into that event," John explained.

"How much money?" Katie ran the totals for King's share of the winner's purse in her head.

John unfolded the cooling-out blanket and threw it over King's back. "More money than this colt has won."

Katie was downhearted. She knew King was good. Today's race had proved how much heart he had. Now she would have to content herself with running him in the smaller races. Maybe someday, one of King's babies would be able to compete in the Kentucky Derby.

John broke into her thoughts. "Don't look so sullen, girl. This horse just ran a heck of a race. You've got a lot to be proud of. You two have come a long way together."

"You're right, John." Katie smiled at him and counted her blessings. King was safe, and their farm was too. She had a lot to be thankful for.

The gate to the test barn clanged shut and Mr. Ellis entered.

"Congratulations, Katie." He extended his hand. "The colt ran a great race. Has John told you his surprise yet?"

She looked to the old trainer. "Surprise? What kind of surprise do you have?"

The rest of their troop arrived, and John signed them into the restricted area.

"Let me give you mine first." Mr. Ellis reached into his pocket and pulled out an envelope.

"What's this?" Katie said as she ripped it open.

"Those are Jester's lease papers. He wasn't doing so well in Cindy's care, so I'm giving him back to you a little early. She'll have to make do with her old horse until she learns how to take responsibility for herself and the animal."

"Thank you!" Katie gave the stable owner a big hug. "This day couldn't be any better." Jason winked at her, and she giggled happily.

"I wouldn't say that." John stepped forward and tipped his hat at a jaunty angle. "I might be able to improve it a bit," he drawled, trying to drag out the suspense.

"Come on, John, we're dying to know!" Mrs. Durham cut in.

"Well…" the old trainer began. "It seems there was this little gal who had a lot of faith in this crooked-legged colt. She worked real hard with him and turned the colt into a great racehorse. She unknowingly inspired a foolish old man to invest some of his retirement savings on the preliminary entry fees for a big race in Kentucky."

"You didn't!" Katie squealed.

"I did." John shut off the hot-walker and gave King a sip of water. "Get over here and pat the horse that's taking us all to the Kentucky Derby."

"I can't believe it!" Katie moved on shaky legs toward the walker.

"We're going to the Derby." The words tumbled from her lips in a barely discernible whisper.

Jason placed a supporting arm around Katie's shoulders. "Not only are we going to the Derby, but I just know we're going to win that race!"

"Not so fast there, lad," John cautioned. "Katie and King have come a long way, and they've accomplished something they can be proud of. King is a great horse, and I think he's got a shot at the Derby, but it won't be an easy race. You're talking about going against the best horses in the world."

"John's right," Mr. Ellis said. "You'll be up against the best Thoroughbreds the sport has to offer. Only one horse can win, but it's an honor just to be in that company."

Katie weighed her thoughts. She knew in her heart that King could do it. He was destined to be a champion. But with all the trouble they'd had just getting him to this race, would they be able to pull together and make it to the Kentucky Derby? A shadow of doubt floated across her mind. She turned her eyes to John.

"Do you think we can do it, John?" Katie held her breath, waiting for his answer. Old John always knew what was best. She trusted his judgment. He hadn't let her down yet.

John smiled his proud, encouraging smile. "I think *you* can do anything you set your mind to, Katie girl." He looked her straight in the eye and patted her shoulder. "Follow your dreams, lassie."

Katie hugged the old trainer, then turned and threw her arms around Willow King's neck, whispering to the eager colt.

"We'll give it our best, won't we, boy?"

Just then the opening chords of Jason's favorite song drifted out from a radio in the test barn office.

"I'd say this calls for a celebration dance," Jason said as he held out his hand to Katie.

Katie looked at his hand, then into Jason's eyes. He held her gaze, and she could feel him willing her to accept his offer. She looked around at all the others standing there. She wanted this dance so badly. She knew it by heart, but if she messed it up, she'd have an audience of all the people she loved the most witness her inadequacy.

King nickered and shoved her with his nose, as if to push her toward Jason. In the seconds that everyone held their breath, waiting to see if she would accept the invitation, the last few years flashed before Katie's eyes. She remembered how valiantly King had fought for his life on the day he was born and all the courage and determination he had showed since then. How could she do any less?

And if she messed up…?

She looked into the faces of the people surrounding her. These people loved her no matter what. If she fell down, they would pick her up, and she would go on and try again. King had taught her that. Why had it taken so long for her to figure it out?

She smiled and placed her hand in Jason's waiting palm. He moved her into the sweetheart position and guided her into the opening steps of the dance. For the next two minutes, Katie blocked out everything except the foot patterns and the glow of affection on Jason's face.

She didn't even realize the song had ended until everyone clapped. She was still on her feet, and Jason still had all his toes, so she must have done it right. She blinked back the burn of tears. She had done it. She had really done it!

King tossed his head and whinnied. Katie patted his damp neck. "Thanks for the lesson, boy." She dried her eyes on his blanket before she turned to face her family and friends. Jason gave her a wink, and Katie smiled warmly at him. She wasn't good at giving speeches, but everyone was looking at her so expectantly.

"W-well…," she stammered. "I hope everybody likes roses and mint juleps, because we are going to the Kentucky Derby!"

A cheer erupted from the group, and King snorted and danced around at the end of his lead line. Katie placed a steadying hand on his halter. "Easy, King. You best save your energy. We've got a date for the first Saturday in May. Let's go show Kentucky what we're made of!"